IF YOU
WERE
HERE

IF YOU WERE HERE

JENNIE YABROFF

MeritPress

Published by
Merit Press
an imprint of F+W Media, Inc.
10151 Carver Road, Suite 200
Blue Ash, OH 45242. U.S.A.
www.meritpressbooks.com

ISBN 10: 1-5072-0002-1
ISBN 13: 978-1-5072-0002-5
eISBN 10: 1-5072-0003-X
eISBN 13: 978-1-5072-0003-2

Printed in the United States of America.

10   9   8   7   6   5   4   3   2   1

This is a work of fiction. Names, characters, corporations, institutions, organizations, events, or locales in this novel are either the product of the author's imagination or, if real, used fictitiously. The resemblance of any character to actual persons (living or dead) is entirely coincidental.

Many of the designations used by manufacturers and sellers to distinguish their products are claimed as trademarks. Where those designations appear in this book and F+W Media, Inc. was aware of a trademark claim, the designations have been printed with initial capital letters.

Cover design by Frank Rivera.
Cover and interior images © Anna Kutukova/123RF.

This book is available at quantity discounts for bulk purchases.
For information, please call 1-800-289-0963.

Acknowledgments

Thank you to my agent, Adam Schear. Thank you to my editor, Jackie Mitchard, and everyone at Merit Press. Thank you to Carol Paik, Cris Beam, Suzanne Menghraj, Kelly McMasters, Molly Antopol, Chanan Tigay, Ryan Kaufman, Lee Vance, Luke Monaco, Meghan Bryant, Joshua Alston, Zeena Meurer, Jon Cohen, Elizabeth Cuccaro, Steve Meyer, and Elizabeth Belkin—you all helped more than you can know. Thank you to my parents, Mary and Larry Yabroff. Thank you to my family: Jack, Anna, Eleanor, and JB.

PART ONE

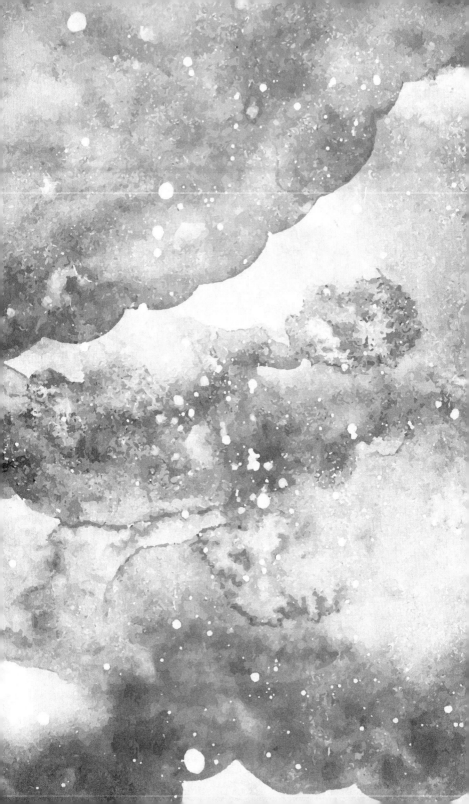

CHAPTER ONE

Once upon a time, I was normal.

Up until fifth grade, I knew how to wear the right clothes and read the right fantasy novels and learn the words to the right songs from the right Disney musicals. If I was never as effortlessly, perfectly normal as Zoe Haley, the most popular girl at Whitman Day, I used to be able to fake it.

When the other kids teased Tomato Face, who had frizzy orange hair and white spit globs in the corners of her mouth and a face that truly was as round as and nearly as red as a tomato, I laughed with everyone else.

When Tomato Face chased the kids around the play yard, threatening to infect us with her mouth-breathing cooties, I ran with everyone else.

When she brushed against me in line for assembly, I rubbed my arm hard and groaned, *Ewww, tomatoitis,* like everyone else.

I never even wondered what Tomato Face's real name was, until the year my mom got sick.

The year it became impossible to keep pretending I was just like everyone else.

• • •

The other kids noticed something was off before I did. On the days I had to go to school in dirty clothes because my mom was too sad to remember to do laundry, the other kids noticed. The day I brought a tin of sardines and three tiny diner packets of marmalade for lunch because my mom hadn't gotten out of bed that morning and my dad didn't know the four acceptable lunch foods (fruit chews, Goldfish, Luna bars, chips), the other kids noticed. The day my mom showed up outside the school, crying, and then just stood on the sidewalk, gripping the iron gate, crying louder, like actual *boo hoos*, when I yelled at her to go home, the other kids definitely noticed.

By the time I noticed, or more accurately, by the time I acknowledged that this was not my mom having a bad day or a bad week but how things were going to be for the foreseeable future, there were only about five kids left who would talk to me.

Then it was winter break, and several things happened:

1: On Christmas morning, one of my presents was meowing. When I opened the box, I found a tiny ball of black-and-white fluff inside. The fluff licked my face, then peed all over my hands. I named him Jujube.

2: A few days later, I was combing my hair in the bathroom when I discovered several strands on one temple had turned pure white.

3: When school started again, the number of kids who would talk to me or sit with me at lunch had gone down to one: Tomato Face, whose real name was Tabitha Smiley and who soon became my best as well as only friend.

CHAPTER TWO

That was five years ago. Life since then has been sucky but tolerable. The years have assumed a predictable sameness some might find eyeball-bleedingly dull, but in which I take a certain comfort. September through June, Tabitha and I spend our weeks attempting to navigate the halls and classrooms of Whitman while incurring as little physical and psychic injury as possible. Weekends, we vegetate in Tabitha's bedroom, eating trans fats, allowing Molly Ringwald, Anthony Michael Hall, and Michael Schoeffling to temporarily suspend our disbelief in the possibility of high school romance, and dreading the arrival of Monday.

Every July and August, I escape the claustrophobia, physical unpleasantness, and barely repressed rage that characterize both summer in New York City and my life in general for my grandmother's mountain cabin in Maine. The cabin is straight-up rustic—no Internet, no phone, no TV—and the nearest town is twenty minutes down the mountain. For two months I have no contact with anyone or anything from what I think of as my real life.

I love it.

The cabin is where I learned to swim, swallowing coppery lake water and thrashing my legs until suddenly, magically, I was propelling myself through a new element. It's where I learned to make scrambled eggs, melting an obscene amount of butter in the heavy cast-iron pan, then swirling the eggs with a dented fork as my grandmother stood behind me, one hand on my shoulder. It's where I am my most peaceful self—not exactly happy, but calm. The air smells like sunbaked pine needles and line-dried pillowcases, and when you wake up in the morning, all you hear are the calls of the jays echoing off the mountains.

When I was really little, my mom used to come to the cabin with me, and my memories of those summers are tinged with sadness, a scrim of cloud over the sunny afternoons I can't quite explain or define. As soon as I got old enough to take the train by myself, I've been coming alone. I float around on a raft in the lake, stay up late trying to beat my grandmother at Hearts, and lie on the porch swing eating potato chips and staring at the sky, wondering what the love of my life, Jake Boylan, is doing.

The best part of being at my grandmother's cabin is how well I sleep. Night after night of deep, black sleep.

The second best part of being at my grandmother's is not having to pretend. Not having to pretend to my parents that I have friends besides Tabitha, that I like school, that I am not a hideous social misfit. Not having to pretend to everyone else that my mom is fine, *fine!*

It's not that I talk honestly about these things with my grandmother. It's that she's never asked.

Until.

One night, after sweeping my side of the table clean of the pretzels we use instead of money, my grandma started shuffling for a new hand of cards, then put down the deck and closed her eyes. She got very quiet, and her breath became fast and shallow, like a dog's. I could see her eyes moving under the lids and her chest rising and falling with each breath. After a few moments she licked her lips and opened her eyes again.

"How's school?" she asked.

"Fine. What did you see?"

"Track is still going well?"

"Track is fine," I said, impatiently. "What did you see?"

"Is everything okay with Tabitha? You're still friends?"

No matter how hot the day is, it gets cold in the mountains at night, but all of a sudden the kitchen felt overheated, stifling and close. "Tell me what you saw," I said.

"Let's make coffee."

"After you tell."

"I'm not sure what it is yet." She got up to put the kettle on. When the water boiled, she poured it into the battered silver coffee press that my great-grandmother brought from Turkey a hundred years ago, took a cigarette from the pack she keeps in the cabinet above the sink, and laid it on the table with a pack of matches. I got down the tiny porcelain cups with the yellow roses painted on the sides, and the tiny matching saucers, and the tiny silver spoons and set them carefully on the table. The tea set is my grandmother's most precious possession—the only thing at the cabin that's not dented, rusty, or chipped. Ever since I was a little girl, I've been terrified of dropping a piece.

My grandmother claims to have the gift of sight—to be able to see the future. She says that in Turkey lots of people have this gift.

My father, whose own mother is from Queens, says my grandmother is a kook.

It's true that some of her interpretations of "sight" are pretty loose, like the time she claimed she saw "water, water everywhere." I got all worried that a pipe had burst in our apartment, or the upstairs neighbors' bathtub had overflowed and their floor had fallen through our ceiling. I made her drive me to town so I could call my dad. Nothing happened, I told my grandma. She kept asking questions until my dad said he had gone swimming at the gym that day. *See*, she said, with a triumphant look on her face.

Still, I can't dismiss her entirely.

After rotating our cups counterclockwise in front of our hearts, we drank our coffee in silence, sipping from the same side of the cup each time. The coffee was maple-syrup-thick and almost as sweet, barely cool enough to drink. When we were done, we put our saucers on top of the cups, turned them over, then put them on the table to cool. My grandmother shifted sideways in her chair and lit her cigarette, exhaling the smoke away from the table so it wouldn't blow in my face. She caught her ashes in her palm, another thing she said she learned from my great-grandmother. I ate a few pretzels from the bag while we waited.

When my grandmother had smoked the cigarette down to the filter, she got up, ran the stub under the water at the sink, then came back to the table and lifted her cup off the saucer and stared at the grounds. She poked them with one wrinkled finger, muttering to herself. My heart started thrumming from the jolt of caffeine. My grandmother believes in magic. Signs, portents, messages from beyond the grave. I don't. I find reality frightening enough as it is. But she was starting to freak me out.

"Oh my God, tell me already," I said.

"Change. Change and loss."

"Oh." I wiped the sweat off my lip with the back of my hand. Probably the next day I would drop a handful of pennies and she would raise her eyebrows at me, tilt her chin significantly. Lost change. I took my own cup off its saucer. "What about mine?"

My grandmother narrowed her eyes. "Water."

"Again with the water?" I couldn't keep the skepticism out of my voice. "This wouldn't have anything to do with the fact you live by a lake, would it?" You didn't need to have the gift of sight to predict a swim in my near future. I put another pretzel in my mouth.

She stared at the grounds hard, ignoring me, and her face clouded. "Not a lake."

"Maybe a pool?" I couldn't help teasing her.

She frowned. "Yes, I think that's right. A swimming pool."

My poor grandmother. She was getting old and forgetful. "That was last year, remember? My dad had gone swimming at the gym?" I patted her hand. The skin was soft and dry.

"No," she said sharply. She pointed to the saucer. "This side here"—she tapped her nail against the edge of the saucer near her—"is the past. This is the future." She tapped the opposite side of the saucer.

I looked at the grounds in her saucer. It was like looking for shapes in clouds. You could see anything you wanted to.

"Do you see it?" She was watching me closely.

"Maybe?" I touched the grounds tentatively with my finger. "Not really."

My grandmother gave a little shrug and got up from the table, taking the saucers to the sink and dumping out the grounds. She turned on the water.

"You're sure everything's okay at school?" She kept her back to me.

"Ugh," I said, letting my head drop against the table.

My grandmother turned to look at me, the water still running. "Something happened."

"Nothing happened." I sat up straight. "Everything's fine. I just hate it, that's all."

I expected my grandmother to nod and go back to the dishes— she knows I'm not exactly in the running for prom queen—but she kept looking at me, hard and unsmiling, like she thought I was keeping something from her.

"Did you and Tabitha have a fight?"

"Not that I know of." I reached up and gave the white streak of hair on the side of my head a little tug.

My grandmother dried her hands on a dishtowel, came back to the table, and took my hands in hers. She looked into my eyes. Her long gray braid, her hand-knit sweaters, and her neroli perfume make her seem like a harmless old hippie, but her eyes are something else. For no reason at all I suddenly felt like I might burst into tears.

"Change is not always a bad thing," she said.

"Did you see something in the coffee grounds you're not telling me?" I chewed on another pretzel, though my mouth was dry and my stomach was tight.

My grandmother narrowed her eyes. "I'm not sure what it is. But I see change and loss close to you."

"And you think it has to do with Tabitha?"

"Maybe Tabitha."

"Or maybe someone else?" The light in the kitchen felt invasively bright. The lingering smoke from the cigarette mixed with the smell of dish soap and clogged my throat.

My grandmother kissed my knuckles, then dropped my hands. We were both thinking the same thing. My mom. I searched her face with my eyes, willing her to say more, but she avoided my gaze and started dealing the cards for another hand.

CHAPTER THREE

That night I couldn't sleep. Probably it was the coffee, which was super strong. Every time I started to drift off, I remembered my grandmother's question about Tabitha, and my eyes snapped open.

The last time I'd seen Tabitha had been the night before I'd left for Maine. As usual, we'd watched *Sixteen Candles*. As usual, we'd said all the lines along with the characters. Also as usual, we'd stuffed ourselves on contraband fudge-covered Oreos, which I'd smuggled into her apartment in my backpack.

Everything had been exactly the same as always until we got to the scene in the movie where Samantha (the incomparable Molly Ringwald) runs out of the school dance, and Ted (Anthony Michael Hall), the geek who's in love with her, finds her in the school auto shop. Ted says that he's been a dork since sixth grade, and Samantha says he could totally change over the summer. She says, *I mean, you could come back next fall as a completely normal person.*

Tabitha paused the movie.

Not as usual.

She sat up straight and put down her Oreo. "She's right, you know."

"Huh?" I had been slowly licking my Oreo, trying to get all the fudge off without making the cookie soggy, and I was in a state of half exhaustion from staying up late and half hyperactivity from the sugar. Not that most of what Tabitha said required my full attention anymore. When you've been best friends as long as us, and your lives are as uninteresting as ours, you tend to have the same conversations. Almost like a script. And I could recite my lines without really hearing myself or her.

"Listen to me, Tess." Tabitha picked up the package of Oreos and threw it in the trash, along with her half-eaten cookie.

"Hey! Maybe I wanted more of those." This wasn't in the script.

"We could come back to school this fall as *completely normal people*." She hooked her fingers in air quotes. Her eyes were wide, and her mouth was hanging slightly open, with flecks of Oreo stuck to the corners.

"And we'd want to do that why?" I asked around a bite of cookie, having given up on licking off all the fudge. My stomach suddenly felt sour.

"It might be fun?" Tabitha lifted a finger to her mouth and began chewing on her nail.

"Stop that." I batted the finger out of her mouth. "Are you saying this is not fun?" I swept my hand dramatically around the room. "We have locally sourced gourmet delicacies, intellectually stimulating culture, high fashion . . ." I gestured down at my *Blondie* T-shirt and pajama bottoms, then over to my filthy Converse, lying by the door.

"And yet."

"It's just 'yet.' 'And yet' is redundant, like saying 'and but.'"

Tabitha rolled her eyes. "*And yet*, I wonder if it might be possible to have a tiny bit *more* fun. Like, if we weren't total outcasts. If we tried to be, you know, popular."

"Like Zoe Haley and her evil bitch Caroline underlings?" I stuck out my tongue and put my hands around my throat, making a gagging noise. "A: no, thank you, and B: not possible."

"Why not?"

"Have you looked in the mirror lately?"

"I love you, too."

"I mean, have you looked at us. Not to mention that we'd need to lose about twenty IQ points apiece and undergo some sort of personality transplant that made us simultaneously fake, mean, and cheerful, like Fascist Barbies."

I was trying to make her laugh, but Tabitha was being very still, which she hardly ever was, and she wasn't smiling. "I'm serious. I don't know if I can do another year of this."

"Another year of what?"

"Of feeling like high school is a party we aren't invited to. Of having less than zero percent of a social life, and even less than less than zero percent chance of getting a boyfriend. My mom is already talking about the junior prom. How are we going to get prom dates if we never leave this bedroom?"

"You want to go to *the prom?*"

"My mom says if you don't go to your prom you'll regret it the rest of your life."

"So, what, you want us to somehow magically transform ourselves over the summer so at the end of the year we can wear foofy dresses and dead flowers on our wrists and stand around a dance floor drinking warm Sprite while some sweaty guys try to hump our legs?" My description of the prom was based entirely on what I'd seen in decades-old John Hughes movies and probably totally inaccurate, but I felt certain the truth, whatever it was, couldn't be any more appealing.

"We could try," she said quietly.

I felt a flash of anger. It was our last sleepover before I left for the summer. Why couldn't we just be companionably bored out of our minds together? "And what if I don't want to?" My voice sounded snottier than I'd intended, practically a dare.

Just then Tabitha's mom came in the room, kicked off her flip-flops, and climbed onto the bed with us. I saw her eyes move from the crumbs on Tabitha's lips to the cookie package in the trash to the last bite of Oreo I was still holding in my hand.

Katie is tiny, dresses exclusively in workout clothes, and is always trying to get Tabitha to lose weight by doing stuff like bringing us bowls of frozen grapes, which she swears taste "just like candy!" (Spoiler alert: They don't.) I wasn't surprised that she was already pressuring Tabitha about the prom—she's been talking about it since we were in junior high. I *was* surprised that Tabitha was taking her seriously. Surprised and annoyed.

Katie and I looked at each other for a moment, and I could see her deciding whether to say anything about the Oreos, but then Tabitha pressed play on the remote, and Katie settled back against the pillows.

It was only after the movie ended, and I was drifting off to sleep with the song that plays over the end credits going through my head, that I realized Tabitha never answered me.

• • •

Had that been a fight? I didn't think so. But now, lying in the narrow wooden bed in my room under the eaves of my grand-mother's cabin, staring at the exposed beams, feeling my heart beat in my chest, I wondered.

What if I was wrong?

CHAPTER FOUR

The longer I lay in bed, the hotter I felt, even though the temperature at the cabin drops into the 40s at night. I kicked off the quilt, turned my pillow to the cool side, and opened a window, but nothing helped. When my head started to throb—dully at first, like someone was jackhammering a mile away and the reverberations were faintly rattling my skull—I knew *it* was happening.

There was nothing to do but wait it out, lying as still as possible as the pounding got louder. When the jackhammer was right inside my brain, I wrapped the pillow around my head to muffle the pain and squeezed my eyes shut as tightly as I could. Tears leaked from the corners of my eyes. My hands and feet felt numb.

I heard my grandmother's words over and over, like a song you get stuck in your brain.

Change and loss.

Water.

Not a lake, a pool.

Finally, just before dawn, the hammering stopped. I took the pillow off my head. Outside, the wind had died and everything was so quiet I could hear the lake lapping against the shore, all the way down the hill. I opened my eyes.

I saw Tabitha on a stretcher.

She looked exactly like herself, except very pale and very floppy, like all her muscles had turned to sand. Her eyes were closed, and her lips were slightly open and blue around the edges. Her hair was wet.

I closed my eyes against the image. When I opened them again, two men in blue jumpsuits were pulling a sheet over her.

When they got to her chin, she opened her eyes and stared right at me.

She said, *This is your fault.*

Then she was gone, and I was staring at the beams of the underside of the cabin's roof, my teeth chattering, my hair damp with sweat.

I jumped out of bed and made it to the bathroom just in time. Up came the pretzels, the coffee, the lentil soup my grandmother had made for dinner. When I was sure my stomach was empty, I drank a glass of water and rinsed my face with shaking hands. I felt the way I always feel after *it* happens—exhausted and drained, every muscle in my body spent and sore. But this time, in addition to the physical ache, I felt something new.

Fear.

CHAPTER FIVE

My mom saw a bunch of doctors over the years after she got sick. The medicine cabinet became hard to close because of all the tan pill bottles with unpronounceable words on the labels. But I never asked what was wrong with her.

She looked tired a lot of the time, and when she was going through a not-bathing period she smelled bad, like a closet that's been shut too long, but I never thought she was going to die. Somehow I just knew she didn't have cancer or anything like that.

And the less I asked my dad about what was going on with my mom, I figured, the less he'd ask about what was going on with me.

I started spending most of my time at Tabitha's apartment.

Even though Tabitha knew about my mom and was always cool about it, I was nervous about having her over. What if she suddenly flared her nostrils and looked around for what smelled, and I knew it was my mom, who hadn't changed out of her nightgown in a week? What if we were listening to music in my room and the song ended and we heard my mom crying in her bedroom through the wall? What if her new medication made my mom so spacey she fell asleep at the table the night I invited Tabitha to stay for dinner?

What if my mom asked Tabitha for Katie's number, so she could ask her out to coffee, and Tabitha had to lie and say her mom lost her phone but she'd pass on the message, which she wouldn't, and for which I wouldn't blame her, because who wants to have lunch with a crazy lady? I know all kids think their parents are mortifying, but with my mom, the potential for disaster was real.

Even when my mom was behaving herself, my dad wasn't exactly a welcoming committee. The first time I brought Tabitha over after school, my dad got a funny expression on his face when he saw her standing in our kitchen, licking the icing off a cinnamon roll. I watched his eyes moving from her face, with her rashy freckles and hanging-open mouth, which I'd learned was the result of her asthma making it hard for her to breathe through her nose, up to the frizzy hair, then down to her hands, with their bitten nails and picked-off green polish. I believe she may have been wearing a necktie that day, part of a brief, misguided attempt to pass off *misfit* as *punk*.

My dad is a lawyer and generally a very logical person—one of his favorite things to say is *Every problem has a solution.* I could see his brain working as he watched her, like, what is the solution to *this* problem?

But later when I asked what he thought of Tabitha, all he said was that he was glad I'd made a new friend. I didn't know if he meant because of what was going on with my mom or because of what was going on at school, and I didn't ask. The only thing that made my unpopularity bearable was believing that my parents didn't know anything about it. I couldn't stand it if my dad suspected otherwise—if he blamed my mom or worse, himself.

CHAPTER SIX

I called Tabitha as soon as I got back from my grandmother's, but she didn't pick up. After I'd left her three messages, she finally texted that she was "super busy" and would just see me at school.

Tabitha was never busy.

"Doing what?" I replied.

She didn't write back.

I tried to convince myself that it didn't mean anything, but the closer it got to the start of school, the less I believed it.

Why wouldn't she talk to me?

• • •

The night before the first day of school, my mom decided to cook dinner. Usually, my dad and I fend for ourselves, which means sometime around nine he looks up from whatever paperwork he's doing and says in a startled voice, *I guess I should feed you?*

The decision to cook dinner meant my mom was having a good day. Good days start with a burst of energy, which expresses itself in mammoth cooking projects or move-all-the-furniture, roll-up-the-rugs housecleaning or once, the decision to take up pottery.

That time, I came home from school and she had bought a kiln. Fortunately, this happened a few years into her illness, so my dad and I knew not to say, *Are you crazy?* (the answer to which, obviously, is *yes*). Instead, we just acted enthusiastic, and when, a week later, she crashed, my dad had a long, quiet (but not so quiet I couldn't hear) phone conversation with the owner of the pottery supply place, who, it turned out, had a bipolar son and took back the kiln and gave us a full refund, even for the clay my mom had bought, which then sat, slowly turning to dust, in a plastic bag in the pantry.

Last I checked it was still there.

This time my mom was in the kitchen cooking by five that evening, and judging by the ingredients on the counter, her menu was only slightly overly ambitious. Spinach lasagna, it looked like, with homemade garlic bread and Caprese salad. Which happens to be my favorite meal. I figured there was probably a Sara Lee pound cake in the freezer, too, where it would stay until just before dessert, since they taste best frozen, covered in chocolate sauce, with just the edges starting to thaw.

As soon as I saw the food, my stomach squeezed itself into a hot, prickly ball.

When my dad called me to come to dinner, I pretended not to hear. After a minute he knocked on my door, then opened it. "Tess? Dinner. Mom cooked."

"I'm not hungry." I kept looking at my phone.

"Tess. Mom cooked."

"You go ahead. I'll come out and pick later if I get hungry."

"Are you sick?"

Sick is a weird word. My mom doesn't feel sick, but she is. I felt sick, but I wasn't.

"My stomach doesn't feel great."

"Just come sit at the table. Mom made your favorites. Maybe you'll feel hungry when you see the food."

Out of nowhere, I got angry. Why did my mom have to pick this night to play the Happy Family Game? Why did she have to get all energized and ambitious on the one day I was counting on her being vague and out of it and not noticing I was practically coming apart from nerves and dread of the next day? How come, just because she decided to act like a normal mother for once, everyone else was supposed to immediately drop everything and play along just so her feelings wouldn't get hurt?

Here's the horrible truth: Sometimes I think that if my mom had a regular, physical illness, even something terrible like cancer, it would be easier. If she were lying in bed too weak to talk one day, she wouldn't be doing cartwheels and saying we should all fly to Paris the next.

And if she got better, she'd be better for real. I wouldn't be holding my breath, waiting for her to crash again. Knowing that no matter how much I wanted to believe this super energized, crazy-fun mom was going to stick around for good this time, she'd go away again.

I didn't say anything. I didn't have to. My dad could see how mad I was. He came over to where I was sitting on my bed and put his hands on my shoulders. I shrugged them off—it was his fault, too, somehow—but he put them back and gave me a squeeze. The squeeze said he understood, and it also said, whatever I was thinking of doing, the only acceptable option was to get up and follow him to the kitchen.

So I did.

The lasagna pan was sitting on an oven pad in the middle of the table. The edges were dark brown, practically burnt, just the way I like it, and the cheese in the middle was still bubbling. The Caprese salad had fresh basil and lots of olive oil. The garlic bread was toasty and buttery.

My mom reached for my plate. Her face was flushed from cooking, and her hair stuck out in frizzy clumps around her face from the steam. She'd put on lipstick earlier, probably before she went to the store, but it had worn off to a thin line around her mouth. Her eyes were shiny. The veins on the backs of her hands bulged beneath the skin.

She used to be an actress, on Broadway and everything, before she got sick and started missing rehearsals and showing up late to auditions and stopped being cast in plays. Every once in a while, someone will come up to her when we're waiting for our drinks at Starbucks or standing on a subway platform and say they saw her as Nora in *A Doll's House*. She always smiles and thanks them, but I think she hates being recognized. Once she pulled me onto the J train, and we rode twenty minutes out of our way before we could transfer to the right train, because she said she couldn't stand there a minute longer listening to how her interpretation of a bored housewife changed some stranger's life.

I've seen my mom's old headshots. She was gorgeous. She still has good bone structure, high cheekbones, and a smooth forehead. But it's like her illness has added a layer of ash to her skin, and I'm not sure you'd call her pretty anymore.

"I'm not hungry."

My mom's face crumpled.

"Isn't lasagna your favorite? Did I get it wrong?"

"No, it is."

My dad was looking at me, like, would it kill you to take a bite, push some bread around your plate?

I picked up my water glass and took a tiny, exploratory sip. I couldn't do it.

"I'm sorry."

"You're not going to eat anything?"

I shook my head. A black fog of self-hatred floated in front of my eyes. The rich, melted cheese smell of the lasagna clogged my nose, making me want to gag.

"At least put your napkin in your lap." My dad's tone said I better not argue.

I picked up my napkin and unrolled it. A pair of small earrings shaped like cats fell on my empty plate.

"For tomorrow," my mom said. "So you'll have a good first day of school." My dad reached across the table and squeezed her hand, then let his hand rest on top of mine for a second before putting it back in his lap.

The earrings were black and white, with tiny rhinestones for the cats' eyes and collars, and tiny painted pink noses. They would have been perfect for an eight-year-old girl who just got her ears pierced. Or an eighty-year-old cat lover with a wacky fashion sense. No sixteen-year-old could have worn them without looking like a total dork. Even Zoe Haley wouldn't have been able to pull them off.

I thought about how I would leave the house wearing them the next morning, and when I met Tabitha on the corner by school I'd act insulted when she laughed. I'd keep pretending I liked them until I saw that tiny flicker of doubt in her eyes, like, what if I really did like the earrings, and she was totally hurting my feelings, and then I'd pretend to be offended that she thought I could possibly like something so tacky. I'd explain, as I took them out of my ears and hid them carefully in my backpack, that my mom had gotten them for me, and she'd make a sad face for a moment, and say, *That's actually very sweet*, and we'd both be quiet a second, and then she'd say, *But I swear to God, Tess, those are the ugliest things I've ever seen*, and we'd both start laughing. After school, when we were back on the corner, she'd say, *Aren't you forgetting something?* When I looked confused she'd touch her ears and say, *Meow meow*, and I'd take them out of my backpack and put them back on right before I went inside.

Then I remembered none of that would happen because Tabitha hadn't answered my text asking if we were meeting before school in the morning—so I'd probably be alone.

"Thanks," I said. "I love them."

CHAPTER SEVEN

I was standing outside the break room, pretending to study my schedule but actually just trying to look busy until the first bell rang, when I saw the new girl. The new girl was thin, with straight, shiny reddish-brown hair pulled back in a high, swingy ponytail and the orangiest skin I'd ever seen outside, well, an orange. She was smiling nervously, and I felt sorry for her for a moment—it couldn't be easy transferring to Whitman as a junior—before I realized she wasn't new at all.

She was Tabitha.

This was why I hadn't heard from her all summer. She'd been serious about wanting to come back to school as a *completely normal person*.

And while I'd been at my grandmother's cabin, thinking my life was never going to change, she'd been busy changing everything. Her body. Her hair. Her skin. Her wardrobe.

Herself?

Just then she saw me, and her face lit up with a huge smile. I smiled back and raised my hand to wave, my shoulders dropping about an inch with relief. I'd been wrong. Tabitha might look different, but she was still my friend. Everything was going to be the same as it had always been.

I was still smiling as she walked right by me.

"Amanda!" she squealed. "You look AMAZE. I love your shoes! Urban, right? Who do you have for English?"

I couldn't help it, I turned and stared.

Tabitha had her arms around Amanda Price.

The meanest girl in our school.

The girl who once dumped an entire cherry Slushee on Tabitha's head.

Who'd poked me so hard in the leg with a pencil I still had a little dot of lead in my thigh.

Who called us Spazitha and Mess.

Our nemesis. Amanda Price.

And now Tabitha was hugging her.

She saw me staring.

"Oh, hey, Tess." She looked so excited to be seen in public hugging Amanda, for the tiniest second I almost felt happy for her.

"Hey."

She was still hugging Amanda. They were practically slow dancing in the hall.

Finally they disentangled. Amanda turned and looked at me. She looked me up. She looked me down. I looked back. She was orange, too. Maybe she and Tabitha had run into each other at the tanning salon and become instant BFF as they broiled themselves under the lamps like two underfed chickens. Amanda's eyes traveled back up to my face and narrowed. I raised my hand to tug on my white streak, then dropped it.

"Nice earrings."

I scrunched my shoulders, hoping they might possibly rise all the way past my ears, hiding the offending earrings.

Next to Amanda, Tabitha stiffened. She looked at me. Then she looked at Amanda. Then she looked back at me, looked at my face or more precisely, my ears. She clapped her hand over her mouth and started to laugh.

Just then, Amanda yelped, "Zoe!"

Tabitha and I turned to look. Zoe Haley and Jake Boylan had just walked through the doors.

Even from the other end of the hall I could tell Zoe's tan was real, probably from whatever exotic island she'd gone to with her family for the month of August. She looked genuinely happy to be back at school, laughing and smiling up at Jake, who had his arm around her shoulder.

I flinched. It hurt too much to look at him, to look at them, their happiness, their perfect ease with the world and their place in it.

Amanda went screeching toward them, practically pushing Tabitha to the ground in her hurry. Jake stepped back with an amused look on his face as Amanda launched herself at Zoe. Tabitha and I were left standing there staring at each other.

"Seriously, Tess, what's up with the kitty cats?"

"I like cats. What's up with the Extreme Makeover, Fake Tan Edition?" As I said it, I knew—the deep orange was the only shade dark enough to hide her freckles.

"I told you," Tabitha said. "I'm sick of being a loser."

"You didn't tell me you were going to do all . . . this." I gestured helplessly at her.

"I didn't know I needed your permission." Her voice was stilted, and she barely moved her mouth as she spoke.

"Why are you being like this?" I couldn't keep the panic out of my voice.

"You know, Tess, there are more people in the world than you and I."

"You and me," I corrected.

Tabitha looked disgusted. "And you wonder why you don't have any friends."

I didn't wonder, actually. Unlike being a music nerd, which is secretly cool, being a grammar nerd is just nerdy. But I can't help it. When you have Bride of Frankenstein hair, the body of a prepubescent boy, and a years-running standing as Number

One Freak of the school, you cling to any shred of intellectual superiority you can muster.

"I thought we were best friends." I hated how pathetic I sounded.

Tabitha sighed. "We're still friends. It's just . . . things change, okay?"

No. Not okay. My life was hardly perfect, but it had been working.

Mostly because of Tabitha.

As we stood there, I kept looking over her shoulder down the hall, as though the real Tabitha would appear and tell this impostor to get lost. The real Tabitha was chubby, with frizzy hair. Her habit of breathing through her mouth made her look like she was actually panting with eagerness to be liked. It used to make me cringe sometimes, how desperate she was.

Now I was the one feeling desperate.

"You could have at least told me," I said.

"There's no phone or Internet at your grandma's, remember?"

"I've been home three days. Didn't you get any of my messages?"

"Yes, and I texted you. I was busy."

"Doing what?"

She swept her hand from head to hip with a big flourish at the end, like she was a prize on some old game show. "Project Tabitha, obviously," she said, with a little giggle of excitement. It was, for just a second, the old Tabitha's voice, and it made me feel better momentarily. She was still in there somewhere.

"But how?"

"My mom's credit cards mostly. And this diet where you drink a gallon of lemon juice and cayenne pepper each day."

"Gross."

"It worked, though, right?"

I couldn't deny it. "You look like a total Caroline."

Her face, already orange, turned a sunset red with happiness. "Thank you!" She beamed.

"Are you hungry?"

"Starving."

Just then the second bell rang, and Amanda was back at Tabitha's side.

"Do you want to do pizza for lunch?" I asked.

"She has plans," Amanda said, before Tabitha could answer. "Sorry," Tabitha said, with an apologetic little shrug. Amanda smirked at me, loving every minute.

I watched them walk away from me, their ponytails swinging in unison. Even the backs of their arms were that sick orange color.

Suddenly I remembered what my grandmother had seen in her coffee grounds at the cabin and the vision I'd had that same night. A cold, slippery sensation ran down my spine, like someone had put an ice cube down my shirt.

Now I wonder what would have happened if I'd chased Tabitha down the hall, grabbed her arm, and warned her to stay away from Amanda and the rest of the Carolines. Would she have listened? Would it have changed anything?

But I didn't warn her. I didn't tell her about my grandmother's premonition or what I'd seen later that night.

I let her go.

CHAPTER EIGHT

At the end of the week we had a fire drill. Tabitha was standing with the twins, Imani and Isa, on the front steps as we waited for the all clear to go back to class. I'd been avoiding her since the first day of school, spending my free periods in a rarely used bathroom on the fourth floor. But Tabitha saw me staring before I could look away, so I forced myself to go over to them. They all stopped talking when I approached.

"Hey. Do you guys know what day our first practice is?"

Imani and Isa looked at each other. I know twins are supposed to be able to communicate telepathically and it's supposed to be all spooky, but it was obvious what they were thinking: They were deciding if it would be okay to answer me. If Amanda found out, she'd make sure they paid for the transgression. Isa gave Imani a tiny nod, and they said in unison, "It's next Thursday."

"Thanks. That's what I thought."

I was turning away when Tabitha said, "Hi, Tess," all pointed. She barely moved her mouth when she spoke.

"Hi."

"How's it going?"

It was surreal to be talking to her like she was just an acquaintance, like I didn't know what her underwear drawer looked like and what her farts smelled like and the fact that she still wore a retainer at night. It was somehow worse than if she had ignored me altogether, or if she had called me Mess, had accidentally-on-purpose bumped me with her shoulder in the hall like Amanda would do. That might have felt like we were in a fight, like after a few weeks we'd get tired of being mad at each other and make up. But this—this was like we'd never been friends at all.

Then, while I was still trying to figure out how to answer the incredibly fraught question of *how it was going*, Jake Boylan walked up and asked the twins if they'd seen Zoe.

All the breath evaporated from my lungs and my mouth filled with sand. I have loved Jake since the moment he transferred to Whitman Day in the seventh grade, and I will go on loving him until we graduate and go our separate ways, me to whatever misfit arts college takes me, him to the University of Perfection. Even then and forever after, I will love him. He is, as Samantha says about Jake Ryan in *Sixteen Candles*, my ideal.

Like *Sixteen Candles* Jake (Michael Schoeffling), Whitman Day Jake (Jake Boylan) is impossibly gorgeous. Like *Sixteen Candles* Jake, Whitman Day Jake is quiet and mysterious in that way that you know, even though he's popular and athletic, he has a sensitive soul and feels deep, complicated feelings he doesn't think he can share with anyone. Also like *Sixteen Candles* Jake, Whitman Day Jake is going out with the most popular girl in school. In *Sixteen Candles*, Caroline Mulford. At Whitman Day, Zoe Haley. Finally, like *Sixteen Candles* Jake, Whitman Day Jake is at most fractionally aware of the existence of his soul mate, the girl with whom he can share his deep, complicated feelings, the one who understands him so much better than his shallow, conventional, yes, pretty and sweet but ultimately entirely unworthy girlfriend. In *Sixteen Candles*, Samantha. At Whitman Day, (duh) me.

Standing there on the steps was possibly the closest I'd ever been to Jake. I could see the stubble on his cheeks. The way the little blond hairs caught glints of sunlight made my throat hurt. The tag was sticking out from the back of his shirt. If I were Zoe Haley, I would reach over and tuck his tag back in, and my fingers would brush against the back of his neck, which was tan and warm-looking and probably smelled like fresh-baked cookies and world peace.

But I wasn't Zoe Haley, I was me, so I couldn't even focus on the wondrousness of being in the presence of Jake, because Tabitha was standing there waiting for me to tell her how it was going.

"How's what going?" I finally said.

The old Tabitha would have said, *You know, things, life, whatnot,* which is what Ted says to Samantha on the bus in *Sixteen Candles.*

"Ummm, stuff?"

"Life is not whatnot," I said, automatically finishing the quote before I realized she hadn't said her part. At this point Imani was looking at me and Isa was looking at me and oh dear God Jake was looking at me.

"I didn't say it was." Tabitha's voice was strained.

Then Zoe walked up behind Jake and put her hands over his eyes. Without even flinching he grabbed her hands and pulled them down to his mouth and started pretending to eat her fingers. She shrieked and jumped on his back, and he spun her around so that her hair flew out behind her like a shiny gold cape. When he set her down she flipped her hair out of her eyes, then noticed me.

"Hey, Tess," she said, friendly and calm, like she didn't have a care in the world, which, being Zoe Haley, of course she didn't.

Naturally, Zoe is totally beautiful, with dark blonde, frizz-proof hair, seemingly pore-free skin, and a perfect Cindy Crawford mole on one side of her mouth, but her beauty is beside the point. What's truly remarkable is her imperviousness to the social forces that drive the rest of the school with gravitational inexorability. She is the only one of the Carolines who can be nice to an outcast like me without fearing the wrath of Amanda.

I know it's not personal—she is truly nice to everyone, from the school janitor, who she always says hi to and whose kids she asks about *by name*, to the head of the school, Mr. Porter—who I once saw actually blush when Zoe put her hand ever so lightly on his sleeve—but I can't help feeling like we have a special connection whenever we interact, even if she's just handing me a Gatorade after practice or asking to borrow a pen in Spanish. I imagine it's what it feels like to be acknowledged by Oprah or the president. But this time I was too flustered to get all tingly because Zoe Haley had said hello.

"Fine!" I blurted. "It's going fine!"

Imani and Isa and Jake stared at me like I was a baby bird that had been run over by a bicycle—pathetic and also gross.

Zoe was staring at me, too, but not so much in outright disgust as curiosity. Then she did something weird. She lifted her hand and touched the mole on the side of her mouth. At the same time, without thinking about it, I reached up and grabbed my streak and gave it a little tug.

Then Tabitha started laughing. She slapped her hand over her mouth, and I realized why she had been holding her jaw at that weird angle. She was trying to keep her mouth from hanging open like it usually did.

Maybe I should have felt sorry for her, for how hard she was trying to look like her transition to popularity had been effortless, but I was too mad at how she'd humiliated me in front of Jake.

I hated them all with a sudden, clear passion.

The twins for having each other.

Zoe for having Jake.

Tabitha for wanting to have them—dumb, ordinary, popular, nothing-special them—when she could have had me.

Myself for having no one.

The all-clear bell rang. As I walked away, I heard one of the twins say, "Awkward."

"Super awkward," Tabitha agreed.

I didn't hear what Jake or Zoe said, because at that point I made the decision to take a mental health day, and instead of going back to class, I went home, got in bed, and stayed there the rest of the afternoon.

If my mom could do it, why couldn't I?

CHAPTER NINE

My dad stuck his head in my room later that night. I guess I had been crying, and I guess it showed on my face, because he got that *oh, shit* look.

"Sorry, I should've knocked," he said. "Just checking in before I go to bed."

"Thanks." I resisted the urge to wipe my eyes with my hands, which would've been a dead giveaway I was upset. "Everything good with you?"

He shrugged. "First week of school okay?"

"Mmm hmm." I nodded, but as I did a fresh set of tears leaked out of my eyes and slid down my cheeks. I pulled on my white streak to make myself stop.

"Ummm," my dad said, and when I didn't stop, "Are you sure you're okay?"

I nodded furiously, wiping my cheeks. When I got control of myself again I said, "I'm just tired."

"Do you want me to make you a sandwich?"

I shook my head no, crying again. Why is it that when you're upset, and your dad is nice to you, it makes it so much worse? It would've been so much easier if he'd said, *Stop your blubbering and get to sleep.* Instead he just stood there, watching me cry, looking like he wanted to cry himself.

"I'm probably just stressed about school. About classes, I mean," I corrected myself quickly. "Junior year is really important."

My father looked relieved, like, whether or not he actually believed this was the cause of my tears, it was a useful fiction that would save us both the embarrassment of me having to tell him what was actually wrong. "You have nothing to worry about. You're brilliant. You get great grades. You test well. Any college will be thrilled to have you."

"Thanks, Dad." I managed a smile.

"I can go out for bagels in the morning, if you like."

"Sounds great."

"Pumpernickel with olive schmear?"

"Yes, please."

He winked at me. "Sleep tight, kiddo."

"You, too, Dad," I said as he closed the door.

• • •

After my dad left my room I got up and stood in front of the mirror. I braided my white streak, then tucked it behind my ear and pulled the rest of my hair forward, so you could barely see the braid. I took off my hoodie and rolled up the sleeves of my Ramones T-shirt, then tied the bottom in a knot at the back, so it was tight around my waist. I dug a pair of wedge heels out of my closet and was looking in my dresser for a tube of lip gloss when I found a stack of homemade birthday cards from Tabitha, starting the year we were in sixth grade.

I flipped through the cards: bubble letters, glitter glue, puffy stickers, stick-figure Tabithas and Tesses holding hands. "To my BFF in the WWW," one said. *World Wide Web?* I'd asked. *No, idiot, whole wide world.*

For last year's card she'd cut our heads out of a photo and pasted them onto bodies she'd cut from one of Katie's Victoria's Secret catalogs. My face looked much the same as it did today— like the grumpy love child of Sid Vicious and Emily Dickinson— wobbling above an abundantly endowed bikini top. Tabitha's body now actually looked like the underwear model's, minus a few cup sizes. It was her face that had changed, from pudgy, freckly, and happy to skinny, orange, and mean.

I opened the card. Jake's yearbook photo was glued on the inside, with a speech bubble saying, "Happy birthday, Tess, make a wish," which you'd only know is a *Sixteen Candles* quote if you'd seen the movie as many times as we had.

I started to tear the card in two but couldn't do it.

I shoved the stack of cards under a pile of wool socks, then shut the drawer and turned to the mirror, raising my hand in a wave. *Zoe! Oh my God hi!* I whispered, bugging out my eyes and grinning like a maniac.

It was hopeless.

I was hopeless.

I untied my T-shirt, kicked off the wedges, flopped on the bed, and began unbraiding my streak.

Jujube nudged the door open and came in and curled up at the bottom of the bed, and I put my face in the middle of his belly and breathed in his warm, furry smell for a while.

I know it makes me sound crazy to say this, and probably I am, but here goes: Sometimes my cat talks to me. He doesn't open his mouth and say, *Hello, Tess. How are you today?* like some dumb, obviously fake video on YouTube, but I talk to him all the time, and sometimes, when I need it, he talks back.

"I can't do it," I said into his warm stomach fur. "I can't go to school every day and watch her act like a moron just so those bitches will let her hang out with them. Doesn't she know how lame they are? Doesn't she know she's so much smarter and more interesting than them?"

Maybe she doesn't want to be smart and interesting. Maybe she just wants to fit in.

I lifted my head. "But why does her fitting in mean I have to be left out?"

Juju sighed and twitched his ears—the cat version of a shrug.

"Why is she being so mean to me? Why did she have to embarrass me like that in front of Jake?"

Did she embarrass you, or did you embarrass yourself?

I dropped my head again and huffed against Juju's belly, getting fur in my nose. "I embarrassed myself, but it was her fault."

Remembering how she'd stared at me, like I was the most repellent person on Earth, made me angry all over again, and I started crying harder.

"I hate her," I said. "I really hate her."

Jujube nudged me with his head, and I lifted my face to let him lick the tears off my cheeks.

● ● ●

That night *it* happened again.

What do you call it when you see things that aren't there? Dream, vision, fit, hallucination—no word describes the sweaty terror, the dread in my throat, the powerlessness to stop it once *it's* begun. I worry that if I name it, *it* will get harder to ignore, so mostly I try not to think about it. I've never told anyone—not even my grandma, not even after it happened at her cabin. Not because she wouldn't believe me—she, more than anyone, would believe me and would get all excited and insist it means I have the gift of sight, like her. But she also might tell my dad, who'd worry it means I'm going crazy like my mom.

Which I worry about too.

Another reason not to think about it.

I'd pretty much put it out of my mind, but that night, it all came back—the jackhammer headache, then opening my eyes and seeing Tabitha on the stretcher, bloated and cold. Then her looking straight at me and telling me it was my fault.

When I came back from throwing up in the bathroom, I sat in bed, breathing slowly, waiting for my heart to calm down, wondering where the image had come from, wondering what it meant. I told myself it was over, I could sleep now, and everything would be better in the morning, but I couldn't stop thinking about how I'd felt seeing Tabitha under the sheet.

Guilty.

Scared.

But also happy.

CHAPTER TEN

Before fifth grade, we lived on the Upper East Side, just a few blocks from Whitman Day. Then my mom got sick, and my dad had to quit his job at the fancy law firm and take a job at a less fancy firm, where he didn't make nearly as much money but could be home for dinner every night and make my lunch and take me to school when my mom was having one of her bad spells.

For a while my mom was still getting work doing voice-overs for commercials, but then even that stopped. I was glad when her ads went off the air—it was always weird to be watching TV and hear her voice cheerily extoling the magical whitening power of the toothpaste the happy family was passing around onscreen, while next to me on the sofa my mom sat crumpled in her bathrobe, exhaling hot, musty breath whenever she yawned. But between my dad's smaller paycheck and my mom's total lack of one, we couldn't afford our apartment anymore, so we moved across the park to the Upper West Side, to a smaller, dingier apartment we still couldn't really afford.

We also couldn't really afford for me to keep going to Whitman, but when I asked if I was going to go to public school for sixth grade, my dad slammed his fist on the table and said my education was one compromise he refused to make. I'd never seen him so angry. *For every problem there's a solution*, he said, and then he stopped looking angry and started looking overwhelmed and closed his eyes and began rubbing his temples with his fingers, and I worried he was getting sick, too.

Then he opened his eyes. "I promise you, Tess, you will never, *never* have to leave Whitman," he said. "It is an excellent school, you are getting a superlative education, and as long as I can keep providing you that one thing, I will not feel like a complete failure as a father."

When he said that, I made my own promise: that he would never know how miserable I was.

• • •

Then, one day in sixth grade, Amanda had been trying to get me to take a note from her, poking my leg with a pencil and whispering, *Mess, hey Mess.* The harder she poked, the more determinedly I ignored her, until Ms. Alex snatched the note out of Amanda's hand and told me to go see the nurse for the blood running down my calf. I don't know what the note said, and I don't know what Ms. Alex said to Amanda, but at lunch Sophie told me Amanda was going to kick my ass after school.

As soon as the final bell rang, I ran. I ran out of class, I ran down the hall, I ran down the block, and I ran across the park. I didn't stop running until I reached our apartment building on West 79th Street. I don't know if Amanda looked for me or not. But the next day, just to be safe, I ran home again.

After that it was a habit.

I started checking the time on the bank clock on the corner of 79th and Amsterdam, and I developed this weird superstition, like, if I made it past the clock by 3:22, it would mean my mom had had a good day. And then, when I made it by 3:22 and she still hadn't had a good day, it meant I had to do it faster.

3:21.

Then 3:20.

The Whitman track team worked out on the path around the reservoir in the park. One day the coach, Doug, saw me running, my backpack banging against my spine, the skirt of my uniform flipping up over my knees, and asked if I'd ever thought about going out for cross-country.

Track, I soon discovered, is an excellent way of giving my parents the illusion I have a social life and of ensuring my dad continues to feel like he's not a complete failure as a father. When my dad asks how practice was, I can tell him about the girls' plan to steal the coach's stopwatch, and make it sound like I was right there with them, plotting and laughing. I can retell a horrible knock-knock joke I overheard in the locker room, giving the impression Imani told it to me, not to Zoe and Amanda while I was dressing nearby.

As long as I'm careful to substitute the pronoun "we" for "they" when I talk about practices and meets, my dad never needs to know my own teammates barely talk to me, that no one sits next to me on the bus when we go to meets, that the only one who ever says, *Good race* is my coach. As far as my parents know, "we" are one big happy team, not a bunch of girls running together and another girl ("me") running alone.

CHAPTER ELEVEN

Thursday was the first practice of the season. It was hot and humid, the sort of weather that says summer isn't giving up without a fight—terrible running weather. But I was hoping for a hard workout anyway; was counting on Coach Doug making us run twenty wind sprints as a warm-up, so I could go home sore and exhausted and fall asleep immediately and stay that way until morning. But as I walked toward the grassy patch below the reservoir, I saw a couple of new girls sitting with the team.

One of these girls was Tabitha.

Tabitha, who got Katie to give us cab money if our destination was more than four blocks from a subway stop.

Who could, if pressed, muster a brisk trot for a short distance, say, across the street, if an ice cream truck was on the other side.

And who, to my knowledge, had avoided setting foot on the dinky, tenth-of-a-mile track on the roof of Whitman Day her entire eleven years at the school, citing asthma, forgotten gym clothes, and/or menstrual cramps as excuses.

About that asthma: was she allowed to run? Did Coach know she used an inhaler? Was what she was about to do even safe?

If I knew Tabitha, the answers were probably not, definitely not, and she didn't care. All she cared about now was being popular, and if the popular girls did track, Tabitha would do track. I'd have admired her determination, if it weren't ruining my life.

I let out a little groan. I had been counting on practice as the one part of my day where I didn't have to worry about my crazy mom, and I *also* didn't have to worry about my psycho bitch former best friend. Where all I had to worry about was putting one foot in front of the other as rapidly as possible.

And now Tabitha was going to take that away from me, too.

She saw me staring and gave a super fake, instantly evaporating smile, then leaned over and whispered something to Amanda. Amanda looked at me and they both started laughing.

Zoe was sitting on the other side of Amanda, and Amanda fell into her, trying to include her in the hilarity, but Zoe shrugged her off and started retying her shoe. After a minute she glanced over at me. I gave a little shrug and tried to smile, but my lips refused to move more than a sad twitch.

We began with a set of tempo laps around the reservoir. I tried not to think about where Tabitha was, tried to keep my breathing steady and concentrate on my kick, but I couldn't find my gait, and I started gulping air in nervous gasps. There was no breeze, and I felt like I was pushing my way through the hot, heavy air.

As we approached the first curve, someone pulled up on my heel and stayed there. I tried to move to the side to let her pass, but there was another girl drafting on my other side, pinning me in close. I let myself look. On my left, Amanda. On my right, Tabitha.

Then Amanda's voice was in my ear, hissing, "Move it, Mess," and her elbow was in my ribs, and my knee came up into the back of Tabitha's leg while her foot crossed over mine, and then I was down, hard, in the soft gravelly dirt of the path. My palms skidded on the loose rocks as a little cloud of dirt puffed up in my face, filling my mouth with grit.

I lifted my head just in time to see Tabitha looking back at me, her eyebrows raised in surprise, her mouth open. Ahead of her, Zoe's blonde ponytail swished back and forth as she ran on, oblivious. Then Amanda leaned toward Tabitha and said something I couldn't hear, and Tabitha turned and kept running.

I pushed myself to my feet, spit the dirt out of my mouth, and started jogging well behind the pack. Aside from my ripped palms I wasn't hurt, but I felt sick with rage. Anger coiled around my ankles, making me feel like I might trip again. It sat on my back like a pack full of rocks. I tried to concentrate on the prickling pain from the scrapes on my palms and block everything else out, but the rage rode close to my shoulder, whispering what a loser I was, how much everyone hated me, how much I sucked at everything, even running.

With each lap I fell back farther from the team, and with each lap I hated Tabitha a little more.

By the time I made it back to the grass, my lungs were burning and my throat was raw from gulping air. The rest of the team was already well into the cooldown. At least Tabitha looked in even worse shape than I was. Her face was splotched red, her chest heaving beneath her sweat-spotted T-shirt. She wasn't even trying to keep her lips closed as she panted through her mouth.

She spread her legs in a straddle stretch, glanced around furtively, then pulled her backpack over between her legs and stuck her head in. I knew she was sneaking a hit off her inhaler.

Good. Maybe she'd have a full-blown asthma attack and Coach would say she couldn't join the team. Maybe she'd pass out right here on the grass, and the paramedics would take her away on a stretcher. The image made me remember my vision of her with blue lips and wet hair, and I shivered despite the heat of the day.

And then I smiled.

"Wow, apparently the only exercise most of you got over the summer was shoveling French fries in your mouths. That was pathetic." Coach was looking straight at me. "I'm not naming any names, but I'm embarrassed that our guests think that's the best we can do. In fact, the best running I saw today was by girls who aren't even on this team. Yet."

CHAPTER TWELVE

I was washing the cuts on my palms at a water fountain when I heard someone calling my name. Ms. Labos, our guidance counselor, was hurrying toward me across the grass, but her shoes were slippery and her skirt was tight, so she looked like a penguin trying to ice skate. I bent over the water fountain so I wouldn't embarrass her by watching her awkward progress.

"Tess!" She was winded by her jog. "Got a minute?" She paused, catching her breath. "Just getting out of practice?"

"Yep." Obviously. I picked some skin off my palm.

"Oh! Are you okay? That must sting."

"I'll live," I said.

"I didn't know track was a contact sport!"

I smiled weakly. "I just tripped. It's not a big deal."

"Huh." She looked at me like she didn't believe me. Had she watched the practice, seen Tabitha and Amanda trip me? "Well, I'm so glad you're on the team," she went on, when it became clear I wasn't going to tell her what had happened. "Sports are so important. Not that I'm athletic at all, obviously. But I wish I had been when I was your age." She cocked her head. "Hopefully it's not too late."

"I am hopeful," I corrected.

Ms. Labos scrunched her face at me. "Oh, well, thanks for the support. I mean, yes, I probably should join a gym . . ."

"No, I just meant, hopefully is an adverb. You should say, I am hopeful that it's not too late." I blew on my palms.

Ms. Labos stared at me.

I don't know if Ms. Labos is good at her job or not, because I've never gone to her for guidance. She's not that old, but she dresses like your weird, embarrassing aunt, in skirts that hit her at the worst possible place on her shins, and blazers that she insists on buttoning over her stomach, even though it makes the lapels balloon out. She tries to use slang, but it's obvious she's looked up the words on Urban Dictionary—there's always something not quite right about her usage. And she has this huge, stretchy keychain with a million keys on it, like a janitor, so you can hear her coming from all the way down the hall. Basically, she's a loser—I know my own kind when I see one.

"Anywaaaaayz, I think it's great that you do track," she said.

"Thanks." I resisted the urge to tell her it's *anyway*, not *anyways*. "I'm not sure how much longer I'll be on the team, though."

She made a big, stricken face. "You're not thinking of quitting, are you?"

I hadn't been, but it didn't sound half bad. I shrugged.

"Oh Tess, is there something you want to talk to me about? We can go back to my office right now." She jangled her keys. She had a bunch of pendants and toys and figurines on the ring. Maybe this was some guidance counselor trick, like she'd get you to act out all your problems with rubber dice and a little Minnie Mouse doll wearing a cat costume.

It didn't sound terrible, telling someone about what had been happening with Tabitha, about how hopeless everything felt. For years Tabitha and I had participated in the conspiracy of silence about the social hegemony of Whitman Day: Everyone got along, there were no cliques, there was no bullying. The popular kids perpetuated this illusion and the freaks like Tabitha and me— well, we had no choice.

We pretended that kids like us, completely of our own volition, *chose* to have no friends and eat lunch alone and be ostracized by our classmates every time we set foot in the halls. If we never got our pictures in the school paper or the yearbook, if our Snapchats and Instagrams were constantly sabotaged, if we were treated as if we didn't exist as part of the student body, except as both figurative and literal punching bags, clearly we wanted it that way.

I'd always assumed the teachers and staff knew how messed up the school was and just didn't care, but what if they truly had no idea? What if I told Ms. Labos about what was happening with Tabitha and Amanda and she actually helped make things better? At the very least, I could ask her how she'd gotten through high school being such a dork, and when she'd accepted the fact that she was going to be a loser the rest of her life. My eyes filled with tears at the thought of finally telling someone the truth about how hard everything sucked right now.

Ms. Labos put her hand on my shoulder. "Oh, sweetie." She lowered her voice. "Is it something . . . at home?"

"What?" I shrugged off her hand. "No! Everything's fine at home."

She took a little jump backward. "Okay! I'm not trying to pry. It's just that you left school without permission after the fire drill the other day, which is extremely unlike you."

Unlike me? What was that supposed to mean? She didn't know anything about me. I wrapped my fingers in my streak and gave a little tug to calm myself down.

"I just wanted to check in, in case there's anything I should know about." Her voice was all frosty now. "Obviously, you can't just come and go as you wish. And I'd hate to see you do anything to jeopardize your future." She was talking like a robot, like she'd memorized this text from "How to Talk to Students Who Are Screwups." A little cloud of insects was hovering around my face, attracted to my sweat, and I swatted at them impatiently.

"This is such an important year for you, and you have a very promising future ahead of you, if you keep on track. Ha, no pun

CHAPTER THIRTEEN

At home, my mom's good spell continued. Early in the morning I heard her in the bathroom, doing vocalization exercises and brushing her hair, just like when I was little, before she stopped acting. *Buh buh buh, kah kah kah, pah pah pah, guh guh guh,* then tongue twisters. *A tutor who tooted the flute, tried to tutor two tooters to toot.* All the while the brush rasping through her hair, fast and hard, until strands floated straight up from her head, alive with static electricity.

We don't use words like manic or depressed in the house. The farthest we go toward naming what she has is to say Mom is having a good day, or more usually, Mom is having a day, which means bad.

When my mom is having a good day, she can be magical. I never got to see her on stage, but I bet she was an amazing actress, because even now, after everything, when she's having a good day she can convince you of anything. She can convince the stockers at Modell's Sporting Goods—the same guys who act like it is tearing the fibers of every muscle in their legs if you ask them to check for your size in the back room—to push a Ping-Pong table seven blocks, carry it up the steps of our apartment, wrestle it into the elevator, and set it up in our living room.

When she's having a good day, she can infect you with her optimism, her belief that anything is possible, and you start to think all the rules of gravity don't apply to her and won't apply to you either, if you just have faith in her.

When my mom is having a good day, she can talk you into jumping out a window, make you believe you can fly. You go along, because when she's having a good day, she is the most fun person in the world. And then she crashes, pulling you down with her.

• • •

The Ping-Pong table had been my fault.

Mostly my mom didn't seem to notice if I was home or not, but every once in a while, when she was having a good spell, she would get all interested in my life, and ask why I was always going to Tabitha's apartment but Tabitha never came to ours. I didn't want to hurt her feelings, so I usually just made up excuses about Tabitha's apartment being closer to school than ours (true) and Katie being overprotective of Tabitha (false).

That worked for a while, but one time a few years ago she wouldn't let it go. She kept pressing me, kept asking what it was we did at Tabitha's place that we couldn't do at ours. We were sitting on the sofa, where I had been trying to watch TV, and she was sitting too close and kept jabbing me in the arm in a way that was supposed to be playful but actually hurt. I finally got fed up and said, "I don't know, we just hang out!"

"But what do you *do*?" Poke, poke.

"Stuff." I swatted her hand.

"What *kind* of stuff?"

"I don't know. Normal teenage stuff."

"What's normal teenage stuff?" (Poke.) "Come on, I want to know."

I sighed. I was getting annoyed at this act, at pretending she was a lovingly overinvolved mom who was always in her kid's business, and I was her lovingly exasperated daughter, like we were in some commercial for teen vitamins.

"We watch *Sixteen Candles.*"

"We have a TV." She poked me again. "You could watch *Sixteen Candles* here."

"Seriously, quit it!" I pushed her hand away again. "We play games."

"What kind of games?" She moved on to jiggling my arm. "Board games? We have board games." Jiggle, jiggle.

"Not board games." I pushed her hand away again, maybe a bit harder than I meant to.

"Then what?"

I thought wildly. "Ping-Pong."

After Tabitha's parents got divorced, Katie and Tabitha moved to a huge, brand-new apartment building above a Jamba Juice. Their apartment itself is tiny—Tabitha's room is basically a glorified walk-in closet—but Katie likes it because of the "full-service amenities," which translates to a surly doorman and a lame "community room" with fake leather couches and a huge TV and a hot pink Ping-Pong table. Tabitha and I batted the ball back and forth, once, when someone left some paddles lying out.

"Ping-Pong?"

"We're obsessed. We don't eat. We don't sleep. We don't even talk, hardly. We just hit a little white ball at each other. It's super addictive. You should try it sometime."

I assumed it was clear I was being sarcastic, because my mom got quiet after that and didn't bring it up again, and that weekend, when I said I was spending the night at Tabitha's, she just smiled and said, *Have fun.*

But then, months later, after she'd crashed and the doctors had adjusted her meds yet again and she seemed to be entering another good spell, we were at Modell's, shopping for running shoes for me, and she disappeared. At first I thought she had sneaked out for a cigarette, but after ten minutes she was still missing. I wandered around the store, my box of ASICS under my arm, feeling scared and annoyed. Or mostly annoyed that I was scared.

You aren't supposed to lose your mother in a store, it's supposed to happen the other way around, and the one who gets lost is supposed to be five, not forty-five, but nothing ever happens the way it's supposed to with my mom, not even her good days.

I was just about to have them make an announcement—*Tess's mother, your daughter is waiting for you in athletic footwear*—when I saw her taking her credit card back from the cashier with a huge smile. When she saw me she got a guilty expression on her face, then gave me a big hug.

It was supposed to be a surprise, she said, the store was going to deliver it the next day when I was at school. But since I'd caught her, maybe we could talk them into delivering it that afternoon?

Of course we could.

All the way up Broadway, as the stock guys sweated and grunted and shouted at each other to *watch the curb, watch the cars, watch the dog shit*, and refused to meet my eyes, no matter how hard I tried to send them *I'm sorry* looks, my mom danced beside me, gushing about how fabulous life would be with a Ping-Pong table.

Now Tabitha could come over as much as I wanted, she said.

All my friends could come over.

We could have Ping-Pong parties.

Tournaments, with prizes.

She danced back to check on the workers. "How you doing, guys?" She patted one on the arm. "You eat your Wheaties this morning?"

She caught back up with me.

"Family Ping-Pong night!" she said. "We'll order pizza!"

That night, after my dad had gotten home and seen the table and disguised his shock (or maybe by that point had moved beyond being shocked by anything my mom did), and after we played a few games, with my mom continually telling me to stop being so easy on them, to bring my A game, and me making up an excuse about a strained calf muscle, I lay in bed, and for a little while I believed it.

What if Ping-Pong was actually all that was missing from our lives? What if at school the next day I went up to Zoe Haley and the rest of the Carolines and said, *I know this sounds crazy, and I know you hate me, but how about coming over after school for a friendly game of table tennis?*

And they did?

And I got popular?

And it actually made me happy?

And then my mom got happy because I was happy?

My subconscious must've known better, because that night *it* happened. I saw my mom sitting in the bathtub with all her clothes on, rocking and crying while the shower ran over her, and then I saw my dad running around the house taking the knives out of the knife drawer and putting his belts on a high shelf and emptying the medicine cabinet into a shopping bag, which he locked in his toolbox.

The Ping-Pong table went back the next day.

CHAPTER FOURTEEN

When I came out of my room the Sunday morning before our first race, my mom was in the kitchen making pancakes. The peanut butter jar was already on the table, right by my napkin, and a big glass of orange juice, and a dish of sliced strawberries. My traditional prerace breakfast, which my dad usually makes. But this morning he was futzing with the French press, letting my mom do all the cooking. He was humming under his breath, which meant he was either happy that my mom was still in a good period, or nervous that my mom was still in a good period. Or like me, both.

"Morning, sweetheart." My mom waved the spatula at me. Her hair floated around her face, still fluffy from the brush. "How are the legs?"

"Pretty good." I sat at the table. She served the pancakes. I slathered mine with peanut butter. She poured about half a cup of syrup on hers and cut a huge bite with her fork. She shoved the bite in her mouth and cut off another. She shoved that bite in her mouth before she had finished chewing the first. She finished her stack in under a minute and reached for more.

My dad was watching her. I was watching my dad. When my mom was near done with her second stack, she noticed that we'd stopped eating. She put down her fork and said, "What?" We both got busy cleaning our plates.

The rest of the breakfast went fine. My dad teased my mom about her pancake "recipe," which is Bisquick mix and water, and when it was time to clear the table my mom teased him back about his neurosis about stacking dirty plates. I just sat there, listening to their banter, using my upcoming race as an excuse not to help with the dishes.

My dad switched on the radio and started shimmying his shoulders in time as he washed the plates. My mom grabbed him from behind, twirled him around, and waltzed him around the kitchen, just like in every corny romantic comedy ever. I covered my face with my hands and groaned, like I couldn't bear to witness the cheesiness, but I kept my fingers spread so I could peek through.

My mom spun my dad, then let him go and pulled me off my chair. I tried to protest, but I always forget how strong she can be, and she was pushing me around the floor like I weighed nothing, and soon I was laughing, too. My father was leaning against the counter, catching his breath and wiping his eyes. I pushed away from my mom. I wanted to stop before she did.

"My race! I'll miss the bus."

"We can take you," my mom said.

"You're coming?"

She looked at me like I was crazy, like she came to every single one of my races. "Of course we're coming. Get your stuff. We can take a cab."

I looked at my dad.

"The race is in Long Island," he said quietly.

"Cabs don't go to Long Island?"

My father raised his eyebrows, then exhaled. "I guess cabs go anywhere you tell them, if you have money." He looked at me. "Go on, get your stuff. You didn't really want to take the bus with the team anyway, did you?"

No, I didn't. But for a few blissful moments I had forgotten the reason why.

CHAPTER FIFTEEN

The race went like a dream. Not like one of my bad dreams when *it* happens, the ones I wake from sweating and gasping with the covers bunched in my fists. The good kind, the kind you want to never end.

Tabitha was there as an alternate, but I told myself to just concentrate on the running part and turn off the rest of my brain, and for once it actually worked. Apparently the other teams had spent the summer stuffing their faces with French fries, too, because we placed in nearly every race.

When it was time for my event, long distance, my legs felt loose and light and the dirt was soft and bouncy under my feet. I glued my eyes to the back of Imani's singlet and stayed behind her the whole race. I probably could have even passed her at the end, but I was so surprised at how well I was running, and how good it felt, and how light my heart was in my chest, I didn't even think to try.

She was first across the finish line, and I followed two seconds later.

As I crossed the line, I heard my mom and dad shouting my name from one side of the course, and, over on the other side of the course, I saw Tabitha jumping up and down.

I was extraspecially happy for a second, then remembered she was probably shouting for the other girls, not me.

But then in the next second my mom and dad were hugging me and saying how fast I ran and how easy I made it look, and then it was time to get our medals—dinky little plastic disks on ribbons, but cool anyway—and by the time I looked for Tabitha again, she was gone.

I got my stuff and found my mom and dad sitting in the grass.

"That was so exciting!" My mom bounced lightly against the ground. Her legs were covered with pieces of torn-up grass, and there were bare spots in the dirt around her. Her bottom lip looked a little raw, like she'd been chewing on it. "I thought I was going to have a heart attack waiting to see you. But then when you came around the bend, and you were so far in front, and all the other girls were behind you . . ."

"I came in second, Mom, so technically not all the other girls were behind me."

"You did great, kiddo," my dad said. "How did you feel?"

"Good," I admitted. "I felt really good."

"You looked it. And look at your medal!" My mom jumped up to examine the medal and pulled me to her in a tight hug. Her arms felt like iron bars around my back, and I could feel her heart beating through her chest.

Fast.

Too fast.

I closed my eyes.

"You are my magical girl," she whispered into my hair. "You know that, right? My magical, magical girl."

My heart skipped in my chest and for a second my eyes flew open.

She knew about *it*.

But how could she?

"Stop." I forced myself to push her away. "I'm all sweaty and gross."

"You smell fine to me. Now we have to celebrate."

CHAPTER SIXTEEN

We took the train back to Grand Central, then took the 6 uptown to Serendipity 3. It was a splurge, but my mom insisted, saying it was too special an occasion for our usual neighborhood diner. My dad and I decided to share the Outrageous Banana Split. My mom just ordered coffee and a side of fries, but she inhaled most of her fries before they even got cool enough for me to take one, and then started sneaking bites of the banana split when she thought we weren't looking.

I resolved to just let myself be happy, just give in to how nice it felt to be sitting there with them both, my mom acting all sneaky, my dad swatting her spoon and saying, "Cover me, Tess, I'm going in," each time he tried to take a bite himself, the skin on my temples pleasantly tight where the sweat had dried.

My hair was a frizzy disaster, especially my streak, which had come halfway out of my ponytail, and I knew I smelled bad, whatever my mom said, but I didn't care. I'd even kept on the little silver medal.

I hadn't expected to place at all, and even though I'd only come in second, crossing the finish line right after Imani had felt better than I could have imagined. It made me feel like maybe other things were possible, maybe I could surprise myself in other ways.

Maybe the year wasn't going to be a total disaster.

My mom wouldn't crash again.

I'd stop caring that Tabitha had dumped me as a friend.

Maybe?

Then the door opened and first Zoe, then Amanda, then the rest of the team walked in.

My throat closed around the bite of ice cream I was eating.

I was so stupid.

I should have known not to go to such an obvious Whitman hangout. I should have told my parents I was tired and didn't feel like celebrating. I should have said we could have ice cream at home. I'd been feeling so good, I hadn't even thought to be careful. All the happiness drained out of me, melting like the ice cream.

Please, don't let them see me, I prayed. But they were heading right for our table.

I braced myself for Amanda to knock over my water glass or rip the medal from around my neck as she passed. But she just gave me a smug little smile and walked right by.

Possibly she was on good behavior because my parents were there.

More likely, she knew it was bad enough for my parents to see her and the other girls without me, for my parents to know their daughter had been excluded by her own team.

When Zoe walked by she hesitated, like she wanted to stop and say something, but then Priya nudged her from behind so she just smiled at my parents and kept walking.

I exhaled. It could've been worse. I would just have to make up some excuse for my parents about why the team had gone out without me.

Then I saw Tabitha.

"Hey, Tess." Her face was a mask of friendliness. "Hi, Sylvie. Hi, Ben."

"Tabitha!" my mother blurted. "I saw you at the race and realized I haven't seen you since the summer, is that possible? How are you? How was your summer? How's Katie? Come, sit with us!

Have some French fries! It was so nice of you to come to Tess's race!" She paused for a breath.

Tabitha had turned red under her orange tan. I grabbed onto my streak and pulled so hard I got a headache.

"Oh, that's so nice of you, Sylvie." Tabitha pronounced each word carefully, like she was talking to someone who didn't understand English very well. "I'm actually here with some friends. But it's great to see you."

"Oh!" My mom looked confused. "What about later? Why don't you come over for dinner? I feel so bad that Tess is always at your house. Your mother must think I don't feed my own daughter!" She laughed nervously.

"Wow, I'd love to, but I have plans tonight." Tabitha made a fake sad face. She started to put one finger in her mouth, then clasped her hands in front of her chest instead.

Her nails were blue and gold, our school colors. "It's my friend Amanda's birthday." She turned to me. "Congratulations on the race, Tess. Guess I'll see you around."

"Yeah," I stuttered. "See you."

My parents didn't say anything after Tabitha left the table, but my mom stopped trying to steal my dad's whipped cream. After a while she said, "Tabitha looked weird to me. Did she do something to her hair?"

"I guess."

"Did the two of you have a fight?" my dad asked gently. I shook my head, and we all fell silent again.

I could feel my dad trying to catch my eye, but I knew if I looked at him the tears would come, so I just sat there eating my ice cream with my eyes on the table, even though I had lost my appetite and the lump in my throat made the hot fudge burn going down.

I could hear my teammates talking and laughing in their booth. Their voices would get low, and then they'd erupt in a burst of squeals. I was pretty sure I heard Tabitha say *because she's completely nuts!* And then everyone laughed again.

She had to have been talking about my mom.

Unless she was talking about me.

It hurt when she'd stopped hanging out with me at school. It stung when she'd humiliated me in front of Jake. And it sucked when she'd tripped me at practice. But all of that, I could handle. All of that, I could keep to myself. Anything was okay, as long as my parents didn't have to know. All I wanted, all I'd ever wanted, was to protect them from my unpopularity.

Now there was no way they couldn't know.

It was all Tabitha's fault.

I flashed on the image of Tabitha dead on the stretcher. I remembered the night I'd first seen it, the night my grandmother had asked if everything was okay with Tabitha. I'd told my grandmother everything was fine, but had part of me known, even then, that this was going to happen? Known that while I was floating around the lake thinking things were the same as always, everything had already changed? Way deep down, had I known Tabitha meant it when she said she wanted to come back to school as a *completely normal person*; had I understood that meant she was leaving me behind?

I didn't know where the vision had come from.

I didn't know what it meant.

All I knew was, at that moment, I would have given anything for it to come true.

CHAPTER SEVENTEEN

That night when we got home I pretended to still be happy about the race, but as soon as I was alone in my room I threw the stupid silver medal in the trash. If I hadn't come in second, we wouldn't have gone out for ice cream to celebrate, and my parents wouldn't have seen me be shunned by the team, and by Tabitha.

It was Sunday night. The next day would be the start of another week of eating lunch by myself, being smirked at by Amanda and the rest of the popular girls, and trying not to let my parents see how utterly miserable I was.

I couldn't do it.

I braided my streak as tightly as I could and tucked it behind my ear. *Every problem has a solution.* I took out my phone.

Hey, I wrote, *I miss u.* I stared at the words, then deleted them. Too desperate.

What's up? I tried again. Too fake-casual. Delete.

R u mad at me? Pathetic. Delete.

Can we talk? This was stupid.

Jujube nosed open my door and jumped up on the bed with me. "What should I do?" I whispered.

Just call her.

I put one hand in his fur for courage, took a deep breath, and pushed the call button.

"Hey," Tabitha answered on the first ring. I heard the rumble and crunch of street noise through the phone.

"Hey," I said. Then, when she didn't say anything, "It's Tess."

"Oh." Pause. "Hey." She'd obviously answered without looking, expecting someone else.

"I just wanted to say hi. See how you're doing." My voice quavered. Juju started licking my wrist.

"Okay," she said. "Hi."

"That was weird today."

"What was weird?"

"At Serendipity. Seeing you with Amanda and all the Carolines." Juju moved on to licking the palm of my hand, where the scrapes had mostly healed over.

"You shouldn't call them that," Tabitha said primly. "They're my friends now."

"That's what's weird."

"Sorry," she said, not sounding sorry at all.

"What do you mean?"

"What do you mean what do I mean?"

"I mean, are you sorry that it's weird for me that you're friends with them, or are you sorry you're friends with them, or both?" Jujube paused in his licking and watched me, both of us waiting for her answer.

Tabitha sighed. "Ugh, hang on." There was a clattering noise, and then she must have gone inside, because the background noise got quieter. "I'm sorry it's weird for you. I'm not sorry I'm friends with them."

"So it's all working out exactly like you wanted?"

"Hang on." Then, "Double caramel . . . no, wait, change that, just a large peppermint tea, please. Sorry, I'm back. What did you say?"

"I asked if you're happy."

There was silence on the other end. I couldn't tell if she was distracted by paying for her drink or was thinking about how to answer. "I'm happy," she said. I wasn't sure, but I thought I detected a quaver in her voice. "*Really* happy," she repeated, more strongly. Juju and I looked at each other, and he gave his head a slight shake.

"Why don't I believe you?"

"Tess. I am literally dying of happiness."

"I know that's not true."

"You do?" Her voice was soft again, like she was about to confess that she'd gotten what she wanted and realized she hadn't wanted it at all and to admit that her life had been better before. I knew Tabitha well enough to know all I had to do was wait, be quiet, and let her fill the silence. She never could keep a secret long. But I couldn't help myself. I was too hurt. Too mad. Too me.

"You are not *literally* dying," I said. "Unless you are actually having a life-threatening medical emergency, in which case I need to hang up and call the paramedics."

"Ugh! Why do you always have to do that? You know what I mean," she snapped, all the softness gone from her voice. "I finally have a life, you know? I'm actually on my way to Amanda's party right now, so I can't really talk. I think Jake and his friends are going to meet us later."

I lost my breath for a second, hearing Jake's name.

"You had a life before," I said, when I could speak again.

"Making yourself sick on Oreos and watching the same stupid movie five million times is not a life."

"I liked it."

"Don't you think that might be a tiny problem? I swear, if you weren't so negative about everything and didn't act like you were so much better than everyone, people might not hate you so much."

Better than everyone? I widened my eyes at Jujube. "So this is all my fault."

"Sorry, but it kinda is. Actually, you know what? It *literally* is. You could've changed, too. It wouldn't have been that hard. All you'd have to do is pull the stick out of your ass and start listening to what people say instead of just waiting for them to say *who* instead of *whom* so you can correct them and feel all superior."

"Right. Maybe it was easy for you, since you had no personality to begin with, but I can't just overnight turn myself into a brain-dead moron following Amanda Price around like a lobotomized puppy with a cheap spray tan."

Juju made a low, warning noise in his throat and put a paw on my hand.

Careful.

Tabitha inhaled sharply. "If that's what you think of me, I don't know why you were friends with me in the first place," she said, her breath starting to rasp. "Was it only because no one else would hang out with you?"

Juju twitched his whiskers. *Well? Was it?*

Yes.

Maybe.

I don't know.

"Of course not."

"Because the only reason I hung out with you was because I felt sorry for you." I could hear the hurt in her voice, under the wheeze of her breath. "And I still do. I feel sorry for you, Tess. You could be normal if you wanted to, but instead you'd rather be a freak."

Juju blinked at me. He and I both knew it wasn't a choice.

"I'd rather be a freak than a pathetic wannabe," I said.

"Great. We both got what we wanted."

"Great."

I heard a sharp whoosh and hiss, the unmistakable, heartbreakingly familiar sound of Tabitha taking a hit off her inhaler. All of a sudden my anger evaporated, and all I felt was sad.

Sad, and weirdly, scared.

Not for myself, but for her.

I looked at Juju.

Tell her. Tell her not to go to Amanda's stupid party. Say you'll come over and you can watch Sixteen Candles *and eat cookie dough and gossip about Jake and everything will be the same as it always was.*

I knew he was right. I knew that was exactly what I should say. I knew, somehow, that more than our friendship was at stake, that Tabitha was in actual danger. I knew that this was my chance to save her, and if I didn't, I'd always wonder how things might have been different if I'd told her not to go.

But I didn't.

Instead, I said, "You know they don't actually like you. You may think you've changed, but under that gross tan and that ugly manicure you're still Spazitha, you're still Tomato Face, and once they figure that out they'll drop you, and I hope you don't think you can come running back to me when they do, because you can't. I just want you to know that, okay? Okay?"

I waited for her to answer, but she was already gone.

CHAPTER EIGHTEEN

That night *it* happened again.

The vision was the same. Tabitha on the stretcher, bloated and wet. The paramedics pulling the sheet over her. Her eyes opening to look at me, right before she said it was my fault.

Afterward, I was left sweating and gasping for air. I felt like someone had been pushing a pillow over my face. I sat up and took deep breaths until my heart slowed. My stomach was roiling. The air in my room smelled like rotting garbage.

My legs were shaking when I stood up, and I had to grab a chair and stand there breathing for a minute while the dizziness passed. Then I ran into the bathroom and threw up.

It had never been this bad before.

I splashed some water on my face and staggered out to the hall. The air outside my room was cooler and thinner, not swampy with dread, and my lungs relaxed as my stomach settled and my head cleared.

I went into the kitchen for a glass of water. My mom was on the sofa in the living room, clicking through the TV channels with the volume down. I stood just outside the room, watching her. She was worrying a piece of her hair, wrapping a curl around her finger then pulling it free, over and over. How long had it been since she'd slept?

Standing there without her knowing, I felt like I had interrupted something private, something I wasn't supposed to see.

For a second I forgot about *it*. Reality seemed equally scary.

My mom looked up.

We just stared at each other for a long moment. She smiled, and I saw the effort it took for her to force her lips to stretch, the skin of her cheeks cracking like drying clay. She took her hand from her hair and held it out to me.

I sat next to her and she put her arm around me. Her skin was burning. I could feel every muscle in her arm, tensed like wire. I put my head on her shoulder.

"Bad dream?"

I nodded. If only I could believe it had been just a dream.

We were quiet for a bit, both staring at the mute television. "How are the legs?" The race felt like a long time ago. "Give me your feet." She grabbed one of my legs and pulled my foot into her lap and began kneading under the big toe. Her grip was so strong I could barely stand it, but I was afraid to tell her she was hurting me.

Jujube was lying in the armchair across from the sofa, and he jumped down and came over and settled in my lap. Feeling his warm weight across my thighs helped me relax into the massage. I took a breath, exhaling the pain.

My mom squeezed up my calves, kneading the muscles. Jujube purred raspingly against my chest. My mom patted my other leg. The first leg did feel looser.

"Are you and Tabitha not friends anymore?" My mom watched her own hands work on my second foot.

In my mind, I saw Tabitha on the stretcher, bloated, drenched, purple-lipped. I shook my head.

"Did something happen?"

"I'm just really busy this year, with school and track and SATs . . ." I gave my streak a gentle tug.

"Seems like she has a lot going on, too."

"Those girls are stupid. I mean, I'm friends with them," I added quickly. "I just don't hang out with them outside of school."

My mom patted my feet and pushed them back to the floor. She grabbed my hands and squeezed, forcing me to look in her eyes. "You're my magical, magical girl, Tess. You know that, right?"

I nodded.

"Sometimes it's not easy, being different. Being special. But it's not all bad."

I nodded again and then started to cry, big, ugly sobs. Jujube made a startled mew.

"What if I don't want to be magical? What if I don't want to be special? What if I just want to be . . . normal?" I whispered the last word, scared to even breathe it out loud. I'd never admitted it before, not to Tabitha, not even to myself.

My mom sighed. "You may not have a choice."

I covered my face with my hands. Was she saying she saw it in me, that same madness, that same despair? Jujube started licking my fingers. I could feel my mom watching me.

"Are you sure you don't want to tell me what that was about at the ice cream place today?"

"Tabitha hates me," I said from behind my hands.

"Why?"

"Because I'm a freak. Tabitha used to be a freak, too, but then she decided to be popular, and now she hates me." I lowered my hands and looked at my mom. She had a faraway look on her face and was slowly petting Jujube.

"Why are you a freak?"

I hesitated.

I could tell her about *it*.

What I thought it meant.

Why I didn't want to be magical or special.

Not if it meant I was crazy.

But then whatever show was on the TV switched to a commercial, and a flare of light illuminated my mom's face, and I saw how tired she looked—not just tired, haggard. Haunted. Like the sickness in her brain was eating her from the inside, sucking all the energy and life out of her, replacing it with a horrible adrenalized poison.

She had enough to worry about with her own insanity, without me telling her about mine.

"I don't know," I mumbled. "I just don't fit in."

My mom took a breath. "Is it," she started, in a tiny voice, "is it because of me?"

I started crying again. Not only did my mom know the one thing I had fought so hard to keep from her, she thought it was her fault.

"No!" I said between my tears. "It has nothing to do with you. It's just the way I am."

My mom pressed her lips together. "I know it would be easier for you if I were more like Katie."

If my mom were like Katie, I wouldn't ever wonder what kind of day she was having. I wouldn't have to think up excuses to keep her away from school. I could have friends over anytime I wanted.

If my mom were like Katie, would I still be a freak?

"Stop. Just please, please stop." I put my hands over my ears and shook my head. It was the closest we'd ever come to talking about what was wrong with her.

What was wrong with me.

My streak throbbed.

Juju made a low noise in his throat.

Tell her. Tell her about it. Tell her what you saw.

I don't have to wonder how things would be different if I'd told her. I know. Everything would have changed. But I didn't.

"It's okay, Juju." I took my hands off my ears and ruffled his fur. He narrowed his eyes at me.

"I doubt Tabitha thinks you're a freak." My mom sounded defeated. "You've been friends a long time."

"I said mean things to her on the phone. Terrible things."

"Can you talk to her? Tell her you didn't mean it?"

"I'll call her tomorrow." Exhaustion overwhelmed me. I just wanted the conversation to end.

My mom unplugged my phone from the charger next to the sofa and held it out to me. "Send her a text. You'll feel better."

Again I saw Tabitha, her hair wet, her skin cold. I took the phone. I wrote, *you're not going to believe this, but I had this very bizarre dream, and you were in it.* It's what Samantha decides to say to Jake at the school dance, and I hoped the *Sixteen Candles* quote would make her think fondly enough of me to at least reply.

I hit send, then waited.

Nothing.

I put the phone on the arm of the sofa.

"Did she write back?"

"Not yet." I pulled a blanket over myself, tucked my feet under my mom's thigh, and turned toward the TV. After a few minutes she raised the volume. Juju curled himself in the space between us, a warm, comforting lump against my butt.

My mom put her arm on my leg, and for a moment, right before I fell asleep, I thought I heard her whisper to me. It may have been the television, but it sounded like she was telling me she was sorry.

CHAPTER NINETEEN

In *Sixteen Candles*, most of the action takes place over a single day and night—the day of Samantha's birthday. Because her sister is getting married the next day, there are a bunch of relatives staying at her house, so she winds up sleeping on the sofa. This is after she's given a pair of her panties to Ted, the geek, so that he can win a bet with his geek friends, and after a bunch of other embarrassing things have happened to her. In the middle of the night, her dad comes in and wakes her up and says he knows they forgot her birthday, and she confesses that she's in love with Jake, and her dad gives her a big, consoling hug.

It's stupid, but this scene always makes me cry. I guess her dad reminds me of my dad—so cool and at the same time so clueless.

Then, when she's cheered up a bit, he says, "When you do find the right guy, don't let him boss you around. Make sure he knows you wear the pants in the family." And it all comes back to her— she gave her panties to a geek, she's in love with Jake, Jake loves Caroline—all the hellish misery of her waking reality.

Sometimes I know how that feels.

When I woke up, my dad was sitting on the edge of the sofa. It felt early—too early for school. I rolled over and pretended to go back to sleep, so my dad would leave and let me have another ten minutes of not having to think about what had happened after the race, not having to think about *it*, not having to wonder why he looked so worried.

"Sweetheart, wake up."

"Five minutes."

"Not five minutes. Now." My dad put his hand on my shin. His voice sounded weird.

Mom. She'd tried to hurt herself. I had been so busy with my crazy hallucinations and my fight with Tabitha, I hadn't paid attention to the person who was truly in danger, the person who had been sitting right next to me on the sofa.

"Nooo." As long as I didn't wake up, as long as I didn't have to hear what had happened, my mom was still okay. Nothing bad had happened to her. I hadn't let her down.

"Sweetheart, there was an accident. Tabitha's dead."

Without opening my eyes, I asked the question, though I already knew the answer. "How?"

"She drowned."

PART TWO

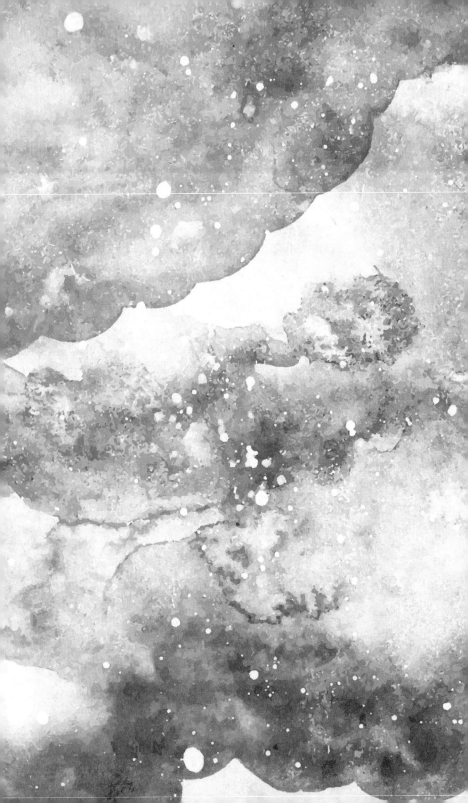

CHAPTER TWENTY

The trees around my grandmother's cabin had lost most of their leaves, and from her front porch you could see all the way down to the lake. In the mornings I wrapped myself in a blanket and sat on the swing, drinking my grandmother's sweet, strong Turkish coffee and watching the mist rise through the naked tree branches.

My grandmother never asked me if I wanted her to read my coffee grounds. When I finished my cup in the morning, she whisked it off the porch and rinsed it quickly in the sink. She usually turned to talk to me as she did this—asking what I wanted for lunch, or if we should drive into town so I could call my dad—as if she were afraid to look herself. It was the closest we came to acknowledging what had happened to Tabitha, to talking about the reason I was there.

· · ·

It hadn't taken long for my dad to tell me all he knew—Tabitha had drowned in the Whitman pool in the middle of the night. School was canceled for the rest of the week. Once my dad had finished talking, he made me a piece of toast we both knew I wasn't going to eat, and we sat at the kitchen table, not looking at each other, waiting for my mom to wake up.

When my mom finally came out of the bedroom, my dad told her what had happened. I pulled Jujube onto my lap and watched my hands running over the fur on his back, so I wouldn't have to see her face when she heard the news.

So I wouldn't have to see if she knew it was my fault.

I heard her, though. She made a gasping, strangling sound, like she'd gotten a bone caught in her throat, and out of the corner of my eye I could see her hands grasping at the air, like she was falling through space.

She knew.

My dad jumped up from his chair and caught her by the arm just as she was starting to collapse. He put his arm around her shoulder and led her back to the bedroom.

I could hear her sobbing through the closed door.

I stayed at the table, staring at my hands.

After a while I put the plate with the toast on the floor, and Jujube jumped off my lap and began licking the butter off the bread. I don't know how long I sat like that, watching Juju, before I noticed I was gripping the butter knife in one fist, the blade against my palm. It hadn't broken the skin, but there was a deep white groove running parallel to my lifeline, the skin on either side red and puffy with blood.

I didn't feel a thing.

The next morning my dad said he thought a change of scene would be good for me, and asked if I wanted to go stay at grandma's.

• • •

It was weird being at the cabin in the fall, with most of the other cabins on the hill boarded up for the season, the lake quiet, preparing to freeze. The sky was low, and the air had a heavy, metallic smell of impending rain—the unsettled energy of the changing season.

At night my grandmother and I played Hearts. I would beg her for one more game, then one more, and when she finally said she had to go to bed, I stayed up reading with my feet propped up in front of her wood-burning stove, willing myself to stay awake as long as possible, terrified of what would happen when I fell asleep.

I barely slept at night, but in the afternoons I climbed the wooden staircase to the second floor, passing framed pictures of myself as a baby and young girl.

I'd try not to look at these pictures too closely as I passed—something about them made me unbearably sad.

At the top of the stairs, I'd go into my grandmother's room, lie down on her bed, pull her blue-and-red handkerchief quilt over myself, and tie a piece of string around one finger. The other end of the string I'd tie to the headboard, then put my hand over my head. I could doze this way for hours, but if I started falling too deeply asleep—deep enough for *it* to happen—my hand would fall, pull on the string, and wake me up.

I saw no reason to ever sleep again.

• • •

On my fourth day at the cabin, a storm came through the mountains, darkening the sky, turning the lake the color of tarnished pewter. We sat on the porch, watching the wind snap branches off the trees and churn up small waves on the lake, then went inside when the rain started to fall, fat sideways drops that pelted the cabin with angry thwacks.

It rained all afternoon, the thunder so loud it hurt our ears. We played Hearts until we ran out of pretzels to bet with, read out loud to each other, finished a crossword puzzle from a weeks-old paper in the pile by the woodstove, and it was still only four o'clock.

My grandmother asked if I wanted to play a board game, and then, without waiting for me to answer, told me to go look in the trunk under her bed. She thought she had a Scrabble board in there, and maybe Backgammon.

I didn't feel like more games—the rain was making me miss my dad, and it was past time for my afternoon nap—but my grandmother was staring at me in a way that made me not want to argue, so I went to her room and pulled out the trunk.

I found the Scrabble board, with ten letters in the bag, and the Backgammon set, missing most of its disks. These were not what my grandmother had sent me to find. Under the games I discovered a photo album, with a cracked, green leather cover that creaked when I opened it, and covered in so much dust my nose immediately clogged.

The first page was a black-and-white picture of a newborn baby, its face tight as a fist, with a downy pouf of black hair on top of its head. Next to the picture was a cut-out column of newsprint, yellowed with age, headlined Birth Announcements. I found my grandparents' names: Korkmaz, Mr. Amir and Mrs. Damla, baby girl, Nihal, on March 31, 7 lbs. 9 oz.

At first I figured I must have had an aunt I didn't know about, before I remembered my mother had changed her name to Sylvia when she became an actress. She was the baby in the picture.

Nihal.

I sat on the floor, looking at pictures of my mother as a girl. My mother feeding a small dog an ice cream cone. My mother in a bathing suit with a ruffled skirt, holding a bucket and shovel. I'd seen some of these pictures before, but I'd never looked at them closely. Now I studied them. In some she scowled at the camera, but in others she smiled brightly, just another happy little girl with unevenly spaced teeth and scraggly braids.

As she got older, her eyebrows grew heavier, and she smiled less, avoided looking straight at the camera. One picture that caught her with her mouth open revealed the glint of braces, and then, for a few pages after that, she smiled constantly, showing her new straight teeth.

Just when I was sure I had glimpsed it, the clue to when she'd known she was different from everyone else, when the crazy had kicked in, I'd turn a page and there would be a happy family photo where her smiling face seemed to say, *No.*

Not yet.

I was looking at a picture of her in her high school graduation gown, her hair long and shiny under her mortarboard, when my grandmother made a noise behind me. I didn't know how long I'd been looking at the album, or how long she'd been watching me.

"She was so pretty."

"She was beautiful." My grandmother sat down on the edge of her bed, then patted the mattress next to her. I got up and sat beside her, spreading the album across both our laps. She looked at the photo. "She didn't always know it, but she knew it here."

"Was she happy to be graduating high school?"

"Are you kidding me? She'd been counting the days."

Suddenly I was full of questions. "Did she always want to be an actress? Was she very, like, dramatic around the house? Like performing soliloquies and stuff?"

My grandmother laughed. "No. Not all. She was quiet at home. The first time we saw her perform, it was a different person. Singing, dancing . . . fearless."

"Huh." I knew what fearless looked like. Fearless scared me. I took a breath. "Was she quiet in a sad way?"

My grandmother shut the album, then put her hand over mine. "Sometimes she was quiet in a sad way. But sometimes you're quiet in a sad way, too, right?"

I nodded. Outside, the rain beat against the window. The dark day had turned into night without my noticing.

"Do you think she . . ." My voice sounded tight and high. I swallowed and started again. "I mean, when she was young, like my age, do you think she knew she was going to go crazy?"

My grandmother pursed her lips together and squeezed her eyes shut. One of the reasons I love her, and one of the reasons I was able to have this conversation with her, was because I knew she'd think about her answer, and she'd try to tell me the truth.

Her answer wouldn't change anything—my mom couldn't have stopped herself from getting sick, and I wouldn't be able to do anything to stop it either, if it was going to happen to me.

If it wasn't happening already.

Still, I needed to know.

Finally she opened her eyes. "I don't like the word crazy."

"Then what would you call it?"

"Your mother has a gift."

"Right, for acting. That's not what I'm talking about."

"It's not what I'm talking about either. Besides the acting, she has a gift. An extra sensitivity to the universe. My mother had it, I have it, your mother has it maybe stronger than any of us. That's the way I think of it. Your father doesn't agree with me, I know. All he believes in are doctors, and pills, and labels—labels on bottles, labels on people . . ."

I nodded, thinking about the way my dad looked at me sometimes, when he lingered in my doorway at night, like he wanted to say something, but then would just ask if I was hungry or needed another blanket. Was he wondering what label to put on me?

"You asked if she always knew," she continued. "I think she always felt different. Not all the time, and for a long time she could hide it or ignore it. She hid it from us pretty well, but I could tell when it was there."

I remembered overhearing my dad on the phone with my grandmother, fierce whispers about hospitalization and it being time to *face facts*. I knew he thought my grandmother could have done more to help my mother, that she should have taken my mother to doctors when she first started showing signs of mental instability. I'd never heard my grandmother's side.

My grandmother bumped me gently with her shoulder. "Do you feel different?"

I took a breath. In the window I could see the reflection of us sitting on the bed, the album between us, my grandmother still holding my hand. Lightning flashed, and for a second I saw the trees outside, black and bent by rain. "I think maybe I have the gift, too," I said.

CHAPTER TWENTY-ONE

I told my grandmother about *it*, about the visions that fill me with misery and terror. Like the night my mom brought home the Ping-Pong table and I had the vision of her crying in the shower while my dad hid the knives and pills. The next day, after we went to return the table, we were standing on the sidewalk, waiting for the light to change, and just as a bus was coming through the intersection, my mom stepped off the curb.

This old man standing next to us threw his arm in front of her, and I grabbed her other arm and pulled her back on the curb, and the man yelled at her for being distracted and not watching the traffic.

But I knew that wasn't what had happened.

She hadn't been distracted at all.

And I also knew that even if my dad hid all the knives and pills and everything dangerous, we still wouldn't be able to protect her from herself.

My grandma listened, nodding occasionally, but mostly watching my face. When I was done telling her what I'd seen and what had happened with Tabitha, it was close to dark in the bedroom.

She shut the photo album with my mom's pictures, put it away, and said we should go downstairs and make dinner. After dinner she pulled out a bottle of thick, purplish liquid and poured us each a small glass. It was raki, she said, a Turkish liquor. I took a small sip. It tasted spicy and sweet and musky, like licorice and crushed grass. I took another sip.

My grandmother drank hers down in one gulp, then closed her eyes and shivered. When she opened her eyes, she told me the name for *it* was *prophetic dreaming*. Then she said there was nothing I could do about my dreams, and they would probably get worse.

Not sleeping wouldn't work—the premonitions would just find another way to express themselves, like I might start having visions even when I was awake.

All I could do was accept the dreams and try to understand them. Maybe I could even use them for good.

I took a swig of my drink and swallowed hard, fighting the burn. I didn't want to use my dreams for good, for evil, for anything.

I just wanted them to stop.

"What good is it to be able to see the future, when I can't do anything to change it?" I said. "Like with Tabitha. I sent her that text, and she drowned anyway." It felt more like a curse.

My grandmother gave me a small smile. "Start paying attention, start writing them down—not just the dreams, but the feelings of the dreams, and what you think about as soon as you wake up. The more you understand the dreams, the more you'll be able to control them."

"What about you?" I said. It sounded more accusatory than I'd meant. "You saw Tabitha drown, and you didn't do anything to stop it."

"I didn't see Tabitha drown," my grandmother said sharply. "I saw a pool, and I got the sense of impending change. Change and loss, I think were my exact words."

"But how can you stand it, seeing the future and not being able to do anything?"

My grandmother smiled at me then, sadly, and shook her head. "But I did do something," she said. "I told *you*."

CHAPTER TWENTY-TWO

School started again that next Monday. Ms. Labos called me into her office during first period. She was sitting on a scratchy-looking plaid sofa across from her desk, a box of tissues blooming on the side table. A cushion on the sofa was embroidered "I wish I were the person my dog thinks I am." She tossed the cushion on the floor and gestured for me to sit, then asked if she could hug me first. I gave her a tentative pat on the back as she embraced me.

"Are you okay?" Ms. Labos said, once she'd let go and I'd retreated to my side of the sofa.

No answer was safe. "I don't know?"

Ms. Labos smiled. She looked very pale under her makeup, but I could tell she was trying to make her mouth look kind, and like she had everything under control.

"Of course you're not okay. None of us are. Can I get you anything? Water? Coffee? No, you don't drink coffee. Or probably you do, but I shouldn't give you any." She kept smoothing her hands over her knees and tugging at the hem of her skirt.

"I'm okay."

"I've been calling you. Did you get my messages?"

"I lost my phone." I hadn't seen it since the night Tabitha died, when I'd been sitting on the sofa and my mom told me to text her. I'd figured Jujube had knocked it into the gap between the sofa and the wall, and to retrieve it I'd have to move the sofa and roll back the carpet, and then I'd gone to my grandmother's, where there's no cell-phone reception anyway. The truth was, I didn't want to find it and see that last, pathetic message I'd sent her, the dumb *Sixteen Candles* quote that she'd never answered. If I had written something else, maybe she'd still be alive.

Ms. Labos nodded absently.

I took a breath. "Am I in trouble?"

"Oh my God, no." She put her hands over her mouth. For a moment she sat there, shaking her head, tears streaming down her face. I wasn't sure what I was supposed to do. Would it seem more natural if I started crying, too?

I didn't feel like crying.

Ever since the morning Tabitha died, I hadn't felt anything at all.

Ms. Labos took a deep breath. "Obviously, this is a horrible tragedy, and we're still trying to figure out what happened."

"What did happen?"

"Tabitha and . . ." She paused, like she wasn't sure how much she was allowed to say. ". . . some other girls"—the rest of the popular girls, obviously—"broke into the pool Sunday night. Or technically, Monday morning. At some point Tabitha must have dove into the shallow end and hit her head. By the time the other girls noticed and got her out of the pool, she was unconscious. The paramedics weren't able to save her."

"Dived."

"Yes, she died." Ms. Labos put her hand on my knee.

"No, it's 'dived.' Not 'have dove,' 'have dived.' She must have dived into the shallow end."

Ms. Labos gave me a weird look and pulled back her hand. "Right. Must have dived." Her mouth started quivering again. "There are still so many questions. And we need to find out what happened as soon as possible. We need answers for Tabitha's parents . . . well, for all of us."

I nodded. I had no idea what she was talking about.

"I know Tabitha is your best friend."

"Was."

Ms. Labos closed her eyes, and a few more tears slid out from under the lids. She had cried off all her mascara at this point, and she had inky puddles under each eye. She took a deep breath and let it out slowly. "Right, was." She opened her eyes and looked at me. "You must be in shock."

"I guess so?"

"Anyway, since you are . . . were . . . so close, I just wanted to talk to you one-on-one to make sure you're okay and also to see if there's any information you might have about Tabitha's state of mind. Did she seem different at all to you lately? Was she abusing drugs or alcohol?"

I shook my head.

"Because, see, Zoe and Amanda swear they weren't drinking, and it just seems like such a freakish accident, we want to rule out all other possibilities. It can take up to a month to get the toxicology report from the autopsy, and it might speed things up if the coroner knows what to look for. Do you think it's possible she could have been on something and the other girls didn't know?"

"I have no idea."

"She's your best friend!"

"Was," I corrected again.

A flicker of irritation crossed Ms. Labos's face. "Right, right, *was*. I forgot I was talking to the grammar police. It's just hard to talk about someone who was alive so recently in the past tense."

"No, you don't get it. She used to be my best friend. She's not anymore." Now I was the one who was referring to Tabitha in the present tense. "I mean, she hasn't been for a while. Hadn't been?" I was getting confused. "The last time we really talked was the beginning of the summer."

Ms. Labos gave a startled little shake, and a bit of the color came back in her cheeks. This was familiar to her, talking about friends who hated you, and she immediately looked a million times more comfortable.

"Seriously?" She leaned forward. "I did think it was weird that Tabitha would be hanging out with Zoe's crew. What happened?"

"Nothing happened." I started picking at the nubby cover of the sofa. "We just drifted apart."

Ms. Labos sucked on her bottom lip a minute, then cocked her head.

"Was it about a boy? I think some Whitman guys were at the pool too."

Poor Ms. Labos. She wasn't actually that old—maybe twenty-five or something—but she had that premature spinster look about her, like she already had one too many cats at home and a big bag of knitting in her purse, waiting for the subway ride back to Queens.

I knew that she lived with her parents in Queens, just like I knew that she got McDonald's every day, then hid it in her desk, as if we couldn't smell her French fries and apple pie from down the hall, and it felt odd that she didn't know half as much about me.

"No, no boys."

She must have sensed that the conversation had gotten off track, because she sat up straight and took a breath. "Well, I'm sorry to hear that. I know you two are . . . were . . . *used to be* very close. And even if you had a falling out recently, her death must be hugely upsetting to you, so please don't feel like you have to get through this alone. And again, if you know of anything that might have been bothering Tabitha recently . . ." She cocked her head again, to the other side this time, considering me anew as an idea came to her. "Like, this falling-out you had. If, maybe, she was more upset about that than she let on . . ."

If anyone had been upset it was me, not her. The dumpee, not the dumper. But I started feeling nervous.

"What do you mean?"

She shrank back. "I don't mean anything! We'll know a lot more once we get the final autopsy report." She exhaled. "I just hoped you might be able to help us get answers sooner. You can imagine how hard this is for her parents, not knowing exactly what happened to their daughter."

When Ms. Labos said the word "parents," I saw a flash of Katie standing in the doorway of Tabitha's bedroom, barefoot and wearing her yoga pants. Then I saw my own mom, sitting on the sofa in the light of the TV the night Tabitha died. I started shivering.

When I reached up to touch my streak, my hand was shaking.

"Tess? Are you sure you're okay?" My teeth were chattering too hard to answer her, so I just nodded. But I wasn't okay. And I knew, without having to dream it, that things were only going to get worse.

CHAPTER TWENTY-THREE

On Thursday, Coach Doug emailed that we were still going to the meet that weekend. For the race, we'd all wear yellow armbands, because yellow had been Tabitha's favorite color.

Oh, and, PS: The whole team was sleeping over at Zoe's house the night before. Attendance was mandatory.

I'd never even been to any of their houses. And now I was going to spend the night at Zoe's house. Queen of the Carolines, in her castle.

My first thought was to text Tabitha. I could see the little white bubble of her reply: *O to the M to the G. Must discuss. What will u wear?*

Then I remembered I couldn't text her, because she was dead. And that her being dead was the whole reason I was going to Zoe's house. Which Tabitha would have died to be able to do. Not the dictionary definition of irony, but close.

Getting ready for the sleepover, I thought about how, if Tabitha were still alive and we were still friends, she'd be watching me pack my bag, telling me to bring a camisole and pajama bottoms, because that's what all the popular girls would be wearing, and whatever I did, to not, under any circumstances, take my socks off unless there was some way I could get a pedicure before Friday night, because my toenails were hideous.

For a second I saw her sitting there on the bed, chewing on her index finger. I could smell her vanilla body spray, and I could hear her crazy hyena hiccup laugh.

Then she was gone.

I ended up packing both my pajama top and a camisole. I made sure I was wearing clean socks and put my hair in French braids, which is the best way to hide my streak, but then wound up taking them out because they looked babyish, and it's not like the team didn't already know about my stupid skunk stripe. I brushed my hair hard and braided just my streak, then tucked the braid behind my ear and pulled the rest of my hair forward.

Probably when it was time to unroll our sleeping bags there would be no space for me, and I'd wind up sleeping by myself in another room, while the rest of the team laughed and gossiped and crank-called boys or whatever girls do at slumber parties. It would be like the time the team bus left me at the gas station bathroom on our way back from a meet—the more they insisted they had honestly just forgotten about me, the more apparent it was that it had been intentional.

My dad was working on his computer at the kitchen table, and my mom was napping on the sofa when I came out. Jujube was lying curled around her feet with his eyes closed, but the very tip of his tail twitched when I walked into the room. My dad looked up and saw my backpack and sleeping bag.

"Going out?" he whispered, with a mildly baffled expression. I'd never spent the night at anyone's house except Tabitha's.

"To a track sleepover," I said lamely. I guess I should've asked for permission or something. "It's mandatory," I added. "We're being graded on it. For gym." This last part was a quote from *Sixteen Candles*, not that my dad would know.

"Oh. Then I guess you better go." He peered at me, like he hadn't really looked at me in a while and wanted to make sure nothing had changed. "You doing okay?"

I glanced at my mom. She snuffled under the afghan. We'd barely spoken since I'd gotten back from my grandma's. It was like she was afraid to make eye contact with me.

I guess I was afraid to make eye contact with her, too.

Or with anyone.

I had no idea how I was supposed to act. Should I be wearing all black and crying all the time? It probably made me look guilty, that I wasn't more upset.

Because I was guilty.

Juju looked up from the sofa and blinked at me.

Well, are you?

"Yeah, I'm okay."

"You know if you ever need to talk . . ."

My dad had his work papers spread out all over the table, which still had a sticky spot of jam from breakfast. His glasses were pushed up on his head, and I could see smudges on the lenses. He would stay here working until my mom woke up, and then he'd try to get her to eat something or at least go sleep in the bedroom.

"Don't stay up too late," I said.

"Aren't I supposed to be telling you that?" He coughed a dry little laugh, then glanced worriedly toward the sofa. My mom sighed and turned over, and in that moment I wanted to blow off the sleepover, mandatory or not, and just stay home with them. Like my presence in the apartment would be some magical, invisible glue, holding everyone together. As though as long as we were all in the same room, we all would be safe.

My dad.

My mom.

Me.

CHAPTER TWENTY-FOUR

When Zoe answered the door, I realized she was one of the last people who'd seen Tabitha alive. We looked at each other for a moment like we each wanted to say something but were waiting for the other one to go first. Her face was pale, and her mole looked red around the edges, like she'd been rubbing it. Then the moment passed, and all she said was, "Hi, Tess, come on in. We waited for you to set up our beds."

Zoe's apartment was like something from a magazine. It was a huge loft with tons of windows, and the furniture was all light-colored wood or glass or stone. I immediately became aware that I was covered in cat hair and that my socks, while technically both blue, did not actually match. I wished I could be back at our dark, cramped, low-ceiling apartment, even if it smelled like sleep and cat litter and coffee grounds and the funk of medicine and sadness.

The rest of the track team was sitting on the floor in the living area. The twins, Isa and Imani, were braiding each other's hair. Some girls still had their jeans on, but others had already changed into PJ bottoms and camisoles, and I was grateful to Tabitha's ghost for the fashion guidance.

"Tess is here, guys," Zoe said. Amanda and Priya didn't look up, but Nikki did, along with Sophie and Imani and Emma. Imani gave a little wave, and Isa waggled the elbow of the arm holding one of Imani's braids.

"Okay, how should we do this?" Zoe fiddled with her sleeping bag.

"Why would we do it any different than always?" Amanda asked, still not looking in my direction. "A big circle with all our heads in the middle."

I should have known that the team always had sleepovers before meets, and that the only reason I had been invited to this one was because Coach Doug had forced them to include me.

I had been expecting some small acknowledgment of what had happened to Tabitha. But now I understood there would be no mention of Tabitha or the circumstances of her death. It was bad enough for them having me here, ruining their night with my oppressive freakishness.

"Circle it is." Zoe unfurled her sleeping bag with a flourish. "Here, Tess, there's room next to me."

• • •

We ate pizza and watched TV, and Priya and Imani and Emma complained about how fat they were, while Nikki and Sophie and Isa pigged out on ice cream and Oreos. Priya leaped around the room screaming when she thought she'd forgotten to pack her lucky hairband, and Imani and Isa rolled their eyes at each other while Nikki calmly found the hairband in Priya's backpack. Sophie kept singing the same two lines of an old Madonna song over and over until Zoe told her she was going to have to sleep in the kitchen if she didn't shut up, at which point the song was already so deeply embedded in my brain I knew I'd be humming it the entire next day. Every once in a while, I'd catch Zoe staring at me, but whenever our eyes met she'd just give me a vague, prom-queen smile and look away.

I kept thinking about the scene in *Sixteen Candles* when Ted says to Caroline, "I can't believe you're so popular, acting like this." Was I missing something? I didn't think this was all that fun—or at least not any more fun than watching *Sixteen Candles* and eating Oreos at Tabitha's apartment. I wished I'd asked my grandmother if my mom had had a lot of friends when she was my age, if she'd gone to sleepovers and had boyfriends and been popular. Was I having a bad time because I knew I wasn't wanted and my best friend had just died, or was I having a bad time because there was something fundamentally, irrevocably wrong with me?

Were they crazy, or was I?

I tried to imagine how Tabitha would have acted in my place. She would have had no problem joining in—she'd sing along with Sophie and get all hyper from the ice cream and do something dumb like pull down her pajama bottoms and moon everyone or pretend to make out with Zoe's dog, Rufus. Stuff that, if Amanda did it, the rest of the girls would scream with laughter, but when Tabitha did it, they would look at each other and widen their eyes like they were *so embarrassed* for her.

Tabitha had always tried too hard. She made no effort to hide how desperately she wanted to be one of the popular crowd; she was always making a fool of herself to try to impress them, to make them like her.

Was that what had happened at the pool that night? Had she been showing off when she dived in and hit her head? Ms. Labos had said that by the time they noticed her in the water, she was already unconscious. Which meant they hadn't been paying attention to her.

Or were ignoring her on purpose.

• • •

After a while I became self-conscious about how quiet I was being, and I knew if I didn't say anything soon I would get to the point where I *couldn't* say anything, and then they would think I was even more of a freak than they already did. I told myself I had to say something once every ten minutes. I said,

This pizza's good.

Are there any more Oreos?

I think she should choose Chris.

I like your sweats. Are they Abercrombie?

And then, for my dazzling finale,

Does anyone have any toothpaste I can borrow?

Finally Zoe turned off the TV and said, "All right, ladies, time for bed."

By this point I was exhausted.

I lay in my sleeping bag in the dark, licking the unfamiliar flavor of Emma's toothpaste off my teeth, thinking about how I would tell Tabitha about the night, before I remembered that I would never tell Tabitha anything again.

How long would it take before I stopped doing that?

Before I understood that I didn't have anyone to tell about anything anymore?

I thought about Tabitha in the pool, floating face-down in the shallow end, in the minutes before Zoe and the rest of the girls noticed her. How long had she floated there? When she dived in and hit her head, did she know something bad had happened? Did she assume one of the other girls would rescue her, or did she know she was dying?

Did she think about me?

CHAPTER TWENTY-FIVE

I'd made sure to drink lots of Diet Coke before bed to keep myself from falling asleep and having any dreams, so I was still awake when I heard whispering across my sleeping bag.

"Do you think she's talked to the cops?" It sounded like Nikki, but I couldn't be sure. I squeezed my eyes shut so they would think I was asleep.

"Why would she?" That bossy, scornful voice could only be Amanda's.

"They said they wanted to talk to anyone who had any information."

"They always say that."

"Did you tell them anything?"

"Just what happened. Which was nothing, right?"

"You mean besides Tabitha drowning?" Nikki sounded confused.

"I mean, there was no drinking, no drugs, nothing. It was just a tragic accident."

"That's what you said?"

"Yes, and that's what you're going to say, if they try to talk to you."

"A tragic accident," Nikki repeated. She was quiet for a moment. "But what if they talk to her?" She must've been pointing at me. "How will she know to say that?"

"She doesn't have to say that exactly," Amanda said with mock patience. "She just better not say she suspects anything else." She sighed. "I hate having her here. Coach Doug *cannot* make us include her the rest of the season. I'll quit the team."

Please, God, please, I thought.

"Yeah," Nikki said limply, then after a second, "Me, too."

"We should do something," Amanda said. "Something to make sure she knows to keep her mouth shut and stay away from us."

"You mean, like, put her hand in hot water so she'll pee in her sleeping bag?"

"What are you, ten?" Amanda's voice curdled with disgust. "Anyway, that doesn't even work. I mean something serious." They were both quiet, and I could feel them looking down at me. "What about cutting her hair?" Amanda said.

"Like, shave her head?" Nikki's voice squeaked with alarm.

"Shhh! Not all of it—just her white streak."

"What are you guys talking about?" A third voice joined in—it sounded like Priya.

"We're going to cut Tess's white stripe off."

Priya said, "Why?" at the same time Nikki said, "We are?"

"Shhh!" Amanda said, not answering either of them.

Amanda scooted out of her sleeping bag and began tiptoeing around the room. I lay still, keeping my breathing as steady as I could make it.

"Is she serious?" Priya whispered.

"I can't tell," Nikki whispered back.

"Should we do something?" Priya asked.

"You do something."

"No, you."

It was so hard not to reach up and hold onto my streak. Don't get me wrong. It's not like I love being sixteen years old with a skunk stripe of white hair running down one side of my face. In seventh grade, Tabitha and I bought boxes of Nice'n Easy at Rite Aid—strawberry blonde for her, dusky coal for me. The dye turned my streak purple, and for a month I looked like a factory-reject My Little Pony, until it faded to the point that I just looked like I needed to wash my hair. I've always hated my streak, but now I wanted to protect it.

Amanda must have found some scissors, because I felt her kneeling down on the edge of my sleeping bag. I opened my eyes a slit and saw my streak being carefully lifted away from my head. I was just about to spring up and grab the scissors when a hand came down and took them away from Amanda. I screwed my eyes tight again.

"What are you doing?"

"Teaching Tess not to come to any more of our parties."

"Not cool." Zoe didn't sound particularly surprised or upset, just annoyed at having been woken up.

"Having her here is what's not cool," Amanda said. "And we all have to wear those idiotic armbands tomorrow? She's going to start thinking she's one of us."

"I agree, this totally sucks." Zoe gave a big, long-suffering sigh. "My point is, what if she tells Coach? This is supposed to be team bonding, remember? Coach is being so melodramatic about everything, he'd probably make us all cut off a chunk of our hair in solidarity or something."

"Ooooh," Priya said, "I bet we would get on the *Today* show, like when the boys' crew team shaved their heads when Spencer had dick cancer."

"Testicular cancer," Nikki corrected. "Didn't it turn out to just be a swollen gland, so he wound up not having to have chemo after all?"

"And the rest of the team looked like idiots with their bald heads while Spencer still had his hair," Zoe finished.

"Irregardless, I am *not* cutting my hair," Priya said.

"Regardless, not irregardless," I whispered into my pillow.

"No one's cutting their hair, or anyone else's," Zoe said. "Just chill, guys, okay? We'll do the race, wear the armbands, and this whole bonding thing will blow over in a few weeks." Even though my face was in my pillow, I could feel her looking at me. I wanted to sit up and slap her fake, pretty, pretend-friendly face.

"She's not stupid," she said. "She knows she doesn't belong here. The important thing is to act normal. I mean, sad about what happened, of course. We don't want Coach or the cops asking any more questions, right?"

So the cops had been talking to her, too.

"She's such a freak," Amanda said. "And the way she's trying to act like she's not a freak is even more . . . what's the word?"

"Freaky?" Nikki offered.

"Embarrassing," Amanda decided. "'Ooh, I love your sweats, are those Abercrombie?'" she singsonged in a voice that sounded nothing like mine. "As if. I wouldn't be caught dead in that store."

"Speaking of caught dead, how have we not discussed what Tabitha was wearing that night?" Nikki asked. "It looked like . . . Forever 21."

"More like Forever 16," Amanda said, and they all laughed and then fell all over themselves shushing each other.

•   •   •

After that, I had no problem staying awake. I wasn't shocked that Amanda had tried to scalp me in my sleep—she had done worse to me when I was awake. I would have been surprised if the night had passed without some incident to remind me that, dead Tabitha or no, I was still, and would always be, an outcast.

But I couldn't stop thinking about what Zoe had said about not wanting the cops to ask any more questions. I knew I was responsible for Tabitha's death. But maybe I wasn't the only one.

CHAPTER TWENTY-SIX

When we got to Van Cortlandt Park the next morning, the air was misty and the grass was wet with dew, and beyond the shrieks and laughter of the girls, you could sense a stillness in the woods that almost made you believe you were in the country. I smelled a tang of something woodsy and green over the diesel exhaust of the buses, and I felt excited and nervous and eager to get on the course. I knew I wasn't going to win, but I was looking forward to running hard, maybe throwing a few elbows.

I walked over to a tree and braced my hands against the trunk and started stretching my calves, mostly as an excuse to check out the girls on the other teams. Some of them I recognized from past meets, and of course everyone knew the stars, the girls who got their pictures in the paper and already had scholarships lined up. They walked around shaking out their legs and swigging from their water bottles in a way that let you know they were already far beyond such juvenile exercises as high school meets.

It was a big meet, and there were plenty of girls I'd never seen before. Do you ever do that thing where you look at someone else and think about what it feels like to be in her body, what the air smells like in her nose, what the grass feels like against her bare legs, what she's thinking when she looks at you? Do you ever wish so badly you could be another person, for just an hour, just a day?

I surveyed the other girls, switching legs in my lunges. Were their schools as neatly divided into popular and unpopular kids as Whitman, and if so, were any of them outcasts like me who just happened, by accident, to be on a team with the popular kids?

When I saw a girl in shorts at least two sizes too big lift up her singlet and tighten the drawstring, wipe her nose on the back of her hand, then lick her palm and push her frizzy hair out of her eyes, I knew I had spotted my equivalent.

I whispered, "Number sixteen, red singlet," to myself, so I could try to pass her if we wound up in the same race.

Coach called us back over to the bus and handed out the armbands, which were just yellow ribbons that had been sloppily glued together at the ends. Nikki and Emma immediately made a fuss about them, Nikki complaining that her arm was waaay too skinny for the band, Emma complaining that hers was waaaay too fat, Nikki saying that it was because Emma had muscles as opposed to her limp-spaghetti arms, Emma saying she *wished* she had spaghetti arms instead of her flabby lunch-lady arms, and soon enough, just like they wanted, girls from the other schools started crowding around, asking what the bands were for.

"Our friend, Tabitha. She died," Nikki said.

Now Tabitha was their friend? She would have loved that.

"It was really tragic," Emma added, making the same face she made about cute animals.

"So sad!" one of the other girls said. "What happened?"

"We're not supposed to talk about it," Emma said, dropping her voice and widening her eyes.

"At least not until they get back the autopsy report," Nikki said, dropping her voice, too.

"You mean, like, an overdose?" the girl said.

Emma and Nikki looked at each other. "Sort of?" Emma said.

"We've already said too much," Nikki said.

"Let's just say it was a freak accident," Emma said.

"A *tragic* accident," Nikki corrected.

"Were you guys close?" one of the girls asked.

"Totally," Emma and Nikki said in unison, nodding their heads.

"It's super hard to be here today," Nikki added, "but it's what she would've wanted."

I must have made a noise then, over by my tree, because they both looked at me, daring me to refute them.

"We're dedicating this race to her," Amanda said, joining the group. "This one's for Tabitha."

"For Tabitha," Nikki and Emma echoed. I rolled my eyes, not caring if they saw.

Coach yelled at us to line up. I took my place at the start, smelling shampoo and gum and deodorant and the thin, flowery smell of singlets that had been freshly laundered and the heavier, musty smell of singlets that needed to be laundered, feeling the pulse of anticipation and nerves of all the girls pressed in around me, wanting so badly to give myself over to the sensation of being part of this larger organism, but still knowing that the essential part of me was outside the group.

I looked to my left and saw Zoe take her place. She was staring at me. I heard her voice whispering, *She's not stupid—she knows she doesn't belong here*, and my face went hot. She gave me a tiny nod and a weird smile, then touched her mole. Without thinking, I raised my hand and gave her the finger.

The starting gun went off, and for several blissful minutes all I thought about was running as fast as I could. The course was a 5k, so I let myself go all out, pushing past the other girls, swinging my arms and breathing hard.

Then I started thinking about Tabitha.

The things I said to her on the phone the night she died.

What Amanda said about the cops.

What Emma said, when the girl asked if Tabitha had died from an overdose.

Sort of.

What did *sort of* mean?

At first, thinking about Tabitha and about how much I hated Amanda and Zoe and the rest of my team made me run faster. Then, around halfway through the course, I knew I couldn't hold my pace, and I needed to ease up if I didn't want to fall apart before the finish line.

But something weird happened. My legs wouldn't let me slow down.

Soon my lungs were screaming for oxygen. My eyes went blurry so I could barely see the course, and my throat was raw from gulping for air.

I wasn't running so much as hurtling through space, blind and out of control. My feet weighed fifty pounds each, my thighs were brittle and stiff, like they were pieces of timber that might snap at any moment, but still my stupid legs wouldn't stop pumping.

Slow down, I said to my legs, first in my head, then out loud. *SLOW DOWN.* The girl in front of me turned and gave me a look, like, *you slow down, bitch*, but then she saw my face, which must have shown pure terror, and her expression changed to amazement as I zoomed past her. I couldn't stop, and I couldn't slow down, even though every muscle in my body was screaming.

Just stop, I told my legs, but they weren't listening. I saw a huge branch in the path. I ran straight toward it, hoping I would trip and fall, but just before I got to it, another girl kicked it out of the way. My lungs were folding in on themselves like moths' wings. My vision was black around the edges.

It occurred to me that I was going to die. My heart was going to explode, and I would fall down dead in the middle of the course.

Was this what Tabitha felt like right before she ran out of air and drowned?

Up ahead I saw a red singlet. Number sixteen—the loser girl I'd spotted before the race. I aimed right toward her back. It was going to hurt like hell, colliding with her at this speed, but at least I'd be on the ground and I wouldn't have to run anymore. I concentrated on the one and the six on the back of her singlet, and when I was close enough to see the drops of sweat flying off the end of her ponytail, I closed my eyes. I braced for the impact.

My legs kept pumping.

I opened my eyes.

Number sixteen wasn't in front of me anymore.

That's when I really got scared.

I hurtled around the next bend and saw the finish tape up ahead. Coach Doug was standing there with his mouth open as I sailed through the tape, and the parents on the sidelines looked startled, too. Like a switch, my legs turned off, and I collapsed on the grass and rolled over on my back.

For a while I just lay there, drowning.

Everything was completely silent for what felt like several minutes. Then slowly, everyone started clapping. A few seconds later, I heard the next girl come across the finish line, and soon after that the pack started crossing the line, and I was recovered enough to roll over to my hands and knees and crawl to the sidelines, where I sat with my head between my legs, my back still heaving as I caught my breath.

Then the team was around me, pulling me to my feet, patting me on my back. Amanda stood a little off to the side, watching with her arms folded, like she hated me getting all the attention but knew there was nothing she could do about it. Coach asked me how I'd run so fast, and Nikki said, "Tabitha must have been helping her," and then everyone said, "Oooh" and started saying how spooky it was and showing each other their goosebumps.

I looked down and saw that I had lost my yellow armband. When I looked up again, Zoe was staring at me, not smiling, not frowning, just staring, her mole shiny with sweat, and she didn't look away.

CHAPTER TWENTY-SEVEN

For the rest of the afternoon, I felt like I had the flu. My body was hot, and I felt lightheaded and groggy, but when I lay down in bed, I kept remembering the number sixteen on the girl's back coming up fast, and then being on the other side of her. I had a strange sense of shame, like winning the race was somehow a betrayal of Tabitha. When my dad came home later in the afternoon, I didn't even tell him I'd won.

My mom had stayed in bed all day, so it was just my dad and me for dinner. He made what he calls his infamous spaghetti (because *in* this house, it's *famous*), and by my third helping I was feeling better about what had happened. Maybe the other girls had been right—maybe I had been, if not actually helped by, then at least *inspired* by Tabitha's death. Maybe I was angry enough about what Amanda had tried to do to me the night before that my rage turned into adrenaline. Maybe number sixteen had swerved right when I was about to crash into her—my eyes had been closed, after all, so I didn't actually see what had happened.

I was pushing a piece of bread around my plate, chasing down the last streaks of spaghetti sauce, when the phone rang. My dad got up to get it and came back to the table with a funny look on his face.

"It's for you," he said, handing me the receiver.

"This is Tess," I said, my throat tight, my face already turning red. Probably some kids had found our number in a school directory and were prank-calling to ask if my pubic hair had a

skunk stripe, too, and I was going to have to pretend to my dad
that it was a "friend" calling about "homework."

"It's Zoe. Don't hang up."

I didn't say anything.

"I got this number from the team roster. I've been trying your
phone all afternoon but you never answer."

"I lost it," I said.

"You *lost* your *phone*?"

I suppose to Zoe a lost phone would have been nothing less
than apocalyptic, but the only person who'd ever called or texted
me was Tabitha.

"Yep."

"Can you talk?"

My dad was staring at me. "Not really."

"Can you meet?"

"You?"

"Me."

"When?"

"Now."

Amanda was probably listening in on the other extension, biting
her lip to keep from laughing. Zoe would give me directions to
some nonexistent meeting spot, and I'd spend the night running
around the Upper East Side, cold and lost and humiliated,
unable to admit to myself that I'd been the victim of yet another
of Amanda's pranks, while back at Zoe's house, the team would
be having the real sleepover, the one they'd been denied by my
presence the night before, and they'd be laughing themselves sick
at the idea that I was stupid enough to think Zoe Haley would
actually be seen with me alone in public.

I could hear my dad clearing the table. I knew what the night
held. He'd hang around in the kitchen, pretending to organize the
recycling while I did the dishes, and would finally work up the

nerve to ask me how I was feeling about "the whole Tabitha thing" since I'd blown him off the night before.

I'd insist I was fine. I'd finish the dishes, flop on the sofa, and turn on some reality TV. My dad would look up from his papers every once in a while, watch for a few minutes, and make a derisive comment about how trashy the show was. Jujube would roll over on the carpet and stretch his paws above his head, as if showing he agreed and would change the channel if only someone would give him the remote.

At some point my mom would wander out from the bedroom, and my dad and I would hold our breath while we waited to see if she'd come for something to eat or a glass of water, or if she was walking in her sleep and had no idea where she was.

Neither of us would say anything, but soon after, my dad would ask if I was okay to put myself to bed, like I was nine, not sixteen, and when I'd say *I've been putting myself to bed for seven years*, he'd say, *I know it, kiddo*, and kiss me on the forehead and rub Jujube's belly with his foot, then head into the bedroom after my mom.

I took a breath and told Zoe to meet me at a café in the Village.

CHAPTER TWENTY-EIGHT

The café was filled with people—some tourists, plus NYU kids pretending to study, grizzled-looking Village old-timers, and even a few young families with toddlers running around the tables and the parents trying to look like they were still part of the scene. Zoe was already sitting at a table with a messy, whipped-cream-topped drink in front of her.

When she saw me she gave me a big smile and wave, and I remembered what it had been like to have a friend, before Tabitha had stopped talking to me, before Tabitha had died. In spite of myself, I gave a little smile and lifted my hand for a half wave.

I ordered an iced mocha and sat down opposite Zoe. Her pink lipstick made her mole even more noticeable, and two guys in NYU sweatshirts at the next table were openly checking her out. She leaned forward and licked a dollop of whipped cream off the side of the glass, and the guys raised their eyebrows at each other.

"Thanks for meeting me," she said, ignoring the guys. "I'm sorry about what happened at the sleepover."

"Whatever." Was that all this was about? Perfect Zoe knew I'd heard what she'd said about me and couldn't stand the thought of anyone being mad at her?

"It's not what you think."

"Which part am I confused about, the part where Amanda tried to cut my hair, or the part where you said I knew I didn't belong there?"

"All of it." She took a breath. "I know I said some mean things about you, but it's not how I feel. I don't actually think you're a freak."

"But I am a freak," I interrupted.

"Look, I don't even like most of those girls. They aren't really my friends," Zoe said. Her phone buzzed on the table, but she didn't pick it up.

"Right. You and Amanda have been best friends since second grade." Her phone buzzed again. "I bet that's her right now, making sure I'm not dragging you over to the dork side." I nodded toward the phone.

Zoe took a breath and leaned forward. "I'm not saying I want to be besties or anything. I just want you to know I feel bad. It was my house, and I shouldn't have let Amanda treat you that way."

She lifted her cup to her lip and took a sip, watching me across the brim, waiting for me to forgive her.

"You have whipped cream on your face," I said.

Zoe licked her lips. One of the boys at the next table covered his face with his hands, groaning softly. Zoe turned to them. "I have a boyfriend," she said.

I turned to the boys. "I do, too. Three of them, and they lust wimp blood." The boys looked at me like I was crazy, but Zoe laughed.

"So stop staring at us, or we'll sic them all over your weenie asses," she said, finishing the *Sixteen Candles* quote.

I raised my eyebrows.

"You're not the only one who loves that movie," she said. "You think I don't know why you call us the Carolines?"

My face went hot with embarrassment.

"It's not exactly an insult," Zoe said. "Caroline is the most popular girl at her school, just like me. And her boyfriend worships her, just like my boyfriend worships me."

And Samantha loves Caroline's boyfriend, just like I love your boyfriend, I finished in my head.

"So that's it?" I said, changing the subject back to how I'd been wronged. "You want me to forgive you for the awful things you said about me when you thought I was asleep?"

Zoe looked down, and I could've sworn she truly did feel bad. "Yeah, that's it. I just don't want you to think I'm like that. I've felt awful about it all day. I tried to let you know before the race, but you flipped me off. I ran my worst time ever, by the way."

"Maybe you would've run faster if you'd gotten a better night's sleep," I said, not ready to let it go.

"Maybe." She shrugged. "But you didn't sleep much either, and you kicked ass. You've never run that fast. You must've set a new record for the course."

"The only limit to human accomplishment is human imagination," I said, quoting Coach.

"So you *imagined* yourself across the finish line?"

"No," I admitted.

I was tempted to tell her what had really happened, how I'd felt like I was being controlled by something outside myself, about the way it was like I'd run right through the other girl. I wanted to ask why she'd given me such a weird look before the race and again when I won. But what if she didn't know what I was talking about? She already thought I was a freak.

"Aren't you happy that you won? You don't seem excited or anything." Zoe sounded offended by my lack of enthusiasm. Almost as if she had been responsible. It didn't make any sense. Unless . . .

"Yeah, well, my best friend just died, in case you forgot. I know you all find it all dramatic to pretend you were super close with Tabitha now that she's dead, but I actually lost a friend. Maybe that's why I'm not more thrilled about the race. Or maybe it's because one of my so-called teammates tried to attack me in my sleep the night before."

Zoe rolled her eyes. "Okay. Enough. I've apologized about a million times about the hair thing, and nothing happened, so get over it. And as far as I knew, you and Tabitha weren't even close anymore. Not judging by the way she talked about you."

I winced. Of course Tabitha had said mean things about me to Zoe and Amanda.

"I shouldn't have said that," Zoe said more gently. Her phone buzzed again. "Ugh. It's Jake. Give me a sec."

I looked away to give her privacy and found the NYU guys staring at me.

"Hey," the dark-haired one said. "Can you settle a debate between us?"

"It's a tie."

"Huh?"

"If the debate is which one of you is least likely to get her phone number, it's a tie."

Zoe was typing furiously on her phone. Just the thought that somewhere in the city, Jake's perfect, long, strong-yet-sensitive fingers were typing the texts that were racing across the ether to land in Zoe's phone made me feel all jangly inside.

"Ha," said the blond one. "Sassy. I like it."

"We were just debating where you two go to school. Justin—my friend here, this is Justin—says you look artsy, so you probably go to the New School or Pratt. But I think you look too smart for art school, so my money's on Columbia."

Before I could answer, Zoe slammed her phone face-down on the table with a huff, then turned to the boys. "What's going on?"

"NYU," I said. I turned back to Zoe. "They thought we go to Columbia."

"Eww." She wrinkled her nose. "Do we look like total nerds?"

"I told you," the blond one—Justin—said to the other one. "They're way too pretty for Columbia."

"Yeah, now that you mention it—don't I recognize you from a class? I thought you looked familiar when you walked in," the dark-haired one said to Zoe.

"What about me?" I asked. "Do I look familiar, too?"

The two guys looked at me, then looked at each other. Probably they were sending each other thought texts about which one was going to get to go after Zoe and which one was going to be stuck being nice to me. I've seen beer commercials. I know how these things work.

"Totally," Justin said.

"Totally," his friend echoed.

"Anyway, we were just wondering if two beautiful, obviously intelligent yet not at all nerdy ladies such as yourselves would like to accompany us to a party this evening," the dark-haired guy said.

"We told you we have boyfriends, right?" Zoe said. "Don't you think you're wasting your time?"

"Your friend thinks I am," the dark-haired one said, "but I think otherwise."

"Oh, you do?" Zoe raised her eyebrows.

"For one thing, you're here with each other, instead of these boyfriends. And for another thing, whoever you were just texting made you very angry. Angry enough, I'd wager, to want to teach him a lesson by going to a party with a gentleman more respectful of your worth and character."

"And what about my boyfriend?" I asked.

"Which one?" Justin, the blond one, asked. "I thought you have three."

"I do. But they share one brain. Luckily, I'm not with them for their conversation skills."

Justin laughed. "I think you and I are going to get along just fine. So, come on, let's get out of here."

Going to a college party with two boys we'd just met was exactly the kind of thing Tabitha would have killed to do. She was a just-in-caser: the type of girl who would wear lucky underwear to the movies, just in case we met some cute boys there (we never did). Who would bring extra cookies in her lunch, just in case she wound up being lab partners with a popular girl and wanted to share (never happened). Who kept the nights of the junior and senior proms free, just in case some popular guy broke up with his girlfriend and needed a last-minute date (not a chance). She was always wishing on stars, holding her breath in tunnels, throwing pennies in fountains. Just in case. She honestly believed in magic, believed everything could change in an instant.

I, meanwhile, was a snowball-in-heller. I couldn't even remember what underwear I was wearing, but there was an excellent chance it was white cotton and had at least one hole. I'd stopped thinking there was a snowball's chance in hell anyone would see it a long time ago.

"Why not?" I said to Zoe, with a shrug. After all, I told myself, it was what Tabitha would have wanted.

CHAPTER TWENTY-NINE

The dark-haired guy was named Adam, and it soon became clear that somehow, in the journey from the café to the sidewalk, he and Justin had agreed that Adam would get to try his luck with Zoe, while Justin would be stuck with me. They seemed interchangeable to me—Justin was blond and fair, Adam was dark-haired and tan—but they both had the same bland faces, the same freshman fifteen double chins. They had probably been popular back in high school in whatever suburban towns they were from, but beer and pizza and New York living had dulled the edges of their attractiveness, dampened the sparks of their confidence.

They must have discovered that quick sarcasm is as common here as rats in the subway and were feeling shaky about things under their bravado. Otherwise why would they be out by themselves on a Saturday night and so eager to pick up high school girls?

I doubted they believed we were in college. I doubted Zoe liked Adam either. Why would she, when she had Jake?

• • •

Adam and Justin flagged down a cab, and soon we were zooming across the Brooklyn Bridge. Justin sat up front with the driver, and Zoe was in the middle, between Adam and me. He took out a flask and passed it to her. She took a small swig and handed it to me. I sniffed it, as though I'd be able to smell if it had been roofied, but then I figured that Adam had taken a drink, so it was probably safe, and I took a small swallow.

"I thought we were going to an NYU party," I said as the cab clattered over the cobblestones of Dumbo.

"We are," Justin said, turning around.

"In Brooklyn?"

"Greenpoint. Some guys in our frat rented a warehouse."

"Cool." Zoe's voice sounded tight.

"Are you okay?" I whispered.

"Of course," she whispered. "I just don't cross the bridge that often."

Adam and Justin kept passing the flask back and forth, but after a few more sips I stopped drinking. I've been drunk a few times in my life—one incredibly pathetic New Year's Eve, Tabitha and I mixed champagne, cherry brandy, and vermouth and got drunk and passed out before midnight—but I'm not crazy about the feeling. I could tell Zoe was faking her sips, too.

Soon Justin stopped passing the flask back to us. Adam just ignored us, staring out the window, bouncing lightly in his seat.

The cab stopped in front of a big, rundown warehouse with a faded sign out front that advertised it as a Polish bakery, but judging from the broken windows and peeling paint and music and shouts coming from the building, no bread had been baked in it in a long time.

There was a line to get in. A big, muscly guy in a tank top stood at the front of the line with his arms crossed. Whenever a girl walked up, he'd let her pass, but whenever a group of guys came up, he'd look at his phone first and sometimes wouldn't let them in at all. We sat in the cab for a moment, watching the scene.

"Are you guys on the list?" Zoe asked. Justin hesitated for a second, then jumped out of the cab, opened the door, and pulled Zoe out.

"You're our two-legged invitations, right?" He put his hand on the small of her back and pushed her forward.

She looked at me, still in the cab. I shrugged. She held out her hand and I took it and got out. The cab drove off while Adam was still shutting the door. Zoe took my hand again, and we walked up to the bouncer, who barely glanced at us before moving to the side and gesturing us through the door. Justin and Adam followed.

It was murky dark in the warehouse, about a million degrees, and the music was so loud I could feel it in my ribs. I turned around to ask the boys if they knew where the bathroom was, but they had disappeared.

"So much for our knights in shining armor," I yelled to Zoe.

"What?"

"Those guys. They only needed us to get them through the door."

Zoe's eyes got big. Probably no one had ever ditched her before, and she'd expected Adam to follow her around all night, like Jake.

"What dicks!"

"Did you actually want to hang out with them?"

Zoe shook her head. "They were lame." She looked around the room. Her pink lipstick glowed neon in the black light, and her eyes were wide. "I don't know *anyone* here," she shouted.

Neither did I, but I considered that a plus. Zoe, on the other hand, probably never went anywhere she wasn't guaranteed an adoring crowd. It occurred to me that spending your days in a place where people actively hate you makes most things you do outside of school easy by comparison.

"Do you want to go home?"

She took out her phone, started to look at it, then put it away. "How will we ever find a cab out here? Let's stay a little while and then get an Uber. We can use my dad's account. Do you want to try to find something to drink?"

We found a bar, where a girl with long black braids poured whiskey into red plastic cups. We walked from room to room, sipping the whiskey, shouting at each other things like *Do you need to go to the bathroom?* And *Do you want to see what's upstairs?* But mostly *What? What? What?*

I'd never been to a high school party, so I didn't know how they compared, but if they were anything like college parties, I hadn't been missing much.

We decided to locate the bathroom. We found a long line at the top of the stairs and joined the end. Zoe took out her phone and looked at her texts. I read over her shoulder:

where r u?
4 real, not funny
im worried
fine, im sorry
WHERE R U? U OK?

All from Jake.

This was why she didn't want to leave the party—she was staying out to teach Jake a lesson. Zoe saw me reading the texts and shoved her phone in her pocket.

"He is *such* a child," she shouted.

I nodded and made a sympathetic face. Any time she was ready to get rid of him, I was more than happy to take him off her hands.

When I came out of the bathroom, Zoe was talking to a guy in line behind her. She probably had no idea how amazing that was, that everywhere we'd gone, guys, *college guys*, had wanted to talk to us. I bet she assumed this was what life was like for all girls, that guys lined up to talk to you, that all you had to do was smile to get anything you wanted, that little fairies swept the street of litter before you walked by.

"Your turn," I said.

"Oh, it's okay, I don't really have to go." She smirked at the guy. Only Zoe Haley could talk about peeing and make it sound like she was flirting.

"Then I guess it's your turn," I said to the guy. He looked older—much older—and had slicked-back hair that made him look like a gangster or a politician. Something about him set my teeth on edge. If I'd been Jujube, my fur would've been standing up and my ears would've been flat against my head.

"Actually, I don't have to go either." He and Zoe laughed like this was some private joke between them, like only freaks like me actually emptied their bladders.

The guy's name was Finn. While he went to get us more drinks, Zoe said that he had a car and could drive us back to the city. When I asked about her dad's Uber account, she said it was actually only for emergencies. Besides, Finn had said it was raining, so we might as well at least hang out until the rain stopped. I wasn't sure I agreed, but I didn't want to leave by myself. We were stuck with Finn.

Being stuck with Finn meant standing around the party shouting at each other, unable to hear a word, then following him outside into the drizzle for a smoke, where it quickly became apparent we actually had nothing to say to each other.

Finn still wasn't ready to leave, so we followed him back inside. While we were waiting for him to get us more whiskey, I leaned over and asked how much more Finn would have to drink before it constituted an Uber-worthy emergency. Zoe just shrugged and smiled and shouted that she was having fun. Wasn't I?

No. I was not having fun. But I so rarely had fun, I wasn't sure I would even know what it felt like. I looked at Zoe. She did look happy, bobbing her head to the music, smiling at no one and everyone, utterly at ease. If she'd been out of place when we first arrived, she'd figured out quick how to fit in.

I still couldn't understand why she'd insisted on meeting me. Did she just feel guilty about Tabitha and what had happened at the sleepover? Or was it something else, something to do with what had happened at the race?

Did she think we had something in common?

What if we did?

It might not be the worst thing in the world.

When Finn came back with our drinks, I forced myself to take a big swallow. For another hour or so I stood there, smiling as much as possible, laughing whenever Finn said something to make Zoe laugh. He kept leaning over to whisper-shout things in her ear, putting his hand on her shoulder, leaving it there a little bit longer each time.

"So, are you and Jake breaking up?" I asked the next time Finn went to get more drinks. Zoe reared back, pantomiming shock.

"Of course not!"

"Does Finn know you have a boyfriend?"

She looked at me with mock pity. "Again, of course not."

"Don't you think he's going to be mad when he finds out?"

"What makes you think he'll find out? Look, he'll give us a ride back to the city, I'll give him a fake number, and that will be the end of that. And if Jake spends a night wondering where I am, all the better."

"I guess."

"Don't look so serious, Tess! We're just having fun." There was that word again—*fun*.

"Doesn't he seem creepy to you?" We looked at Finn, nearing the front of the drinks line. A guy jostled him, and Finn snarled at him. The guy said something, and Finn leaned forward aggressively. He reached backward with one hand, like he was going to take something from his waistband, but the guy put his hands up in apology, and Finn dropped his hand. He stood there glowering until the guy turned away and retreated into the crowd.

"Not really. I don't think he's creepy. I think he's just . . . *old*," Zoe said. "Like at least twenty-five."

"Isn't that creepy, then, that a twenty-five-year-old would want to give two sixteen-year-olds a ride?"

"Okay, first, he doesn't know we're sixteen. But second, are you really that naive?"

"I'm just saying, we can still take the subway. I think the G stops somewhere around here."

"God," Zoe said. "Are you always this much of a buzzkill?"

Yes. Yes, I am.

CHAPTER THIRTY

By the time Finn was finally ready to go, the rain had turned into a heavy mist, and the streetlights shone in the oil-slicked puddles. I hesitated before getting into Finn's car, a tricked-out vintage Mustang that looked like something a comic book villain would drive. I could see the green globe of a subway station at the end of the block. It would be cold in the station, and the train might not come for an hour, but we would be safe.

Tabitha wouldn't have worried about being safe.

Tabitha was dead.

I opened the door to the backseat.

As Finn pulled away from the curb, I suddenly felt the whiskey. In the quiet of the car, with the low buzz of Finn and Zoe talking softly in the front seat, everything I had been trying not to think about all night came rushing into my head.

How Tabitha had really died.

Why I'd won the race.

What my mom was doing at that moment.

I pulled my legs up and rested my head against the seat belt and closed my eyes.

Finn's window was down, and cold, damp air blew against my face, but suddenly I started feeling hot. My head began throbbing. Softly at first, then stronger.

I told myself it was just the whiskey, but as tears welled beneath my closed eyelids, I knew.

It was happening.

Tears streamed down my cheeks. I held my head with both hands, moaning softly. My hairline was wet with sweat. My skin burned. If Zoe and Finn were talking in the front seat, I couldn't hear them. The pounding in my head drowned out all other sounds. I couldn't tell where we were going or how long we'd been driving. Everything around me was blotted out by pain.

Then, after what could have been minutes but felt like forever, the pounding stopped, and I started shivering.

I opened my eyes.

I saw Finn in the front seat facing Zoe while she slowly pulled her shirt over her head, her shoulders shaking with sobs. Then Finn reached over and put his hand against the back of her neck and started pushing her head down. His other hand held a knife.

● ● ●

I squeezed my eyes shut against the vision. When I opened them again, we were stopped at a light. Finn was staring straight ahead. Zoe was looking out the window. I could see the on-ramp to the BQE in the distance.

"You need to pull over," I said.

"Are you crazy?" Finn said. "We're in the middle of nowhere."

"I'm going to be sick."

"Can't you just hold it in?"

"Please pull over." I tried to make my voice urgent but calm. "It's an emergency."

"Don't you dare puke in my car. If you're going to be sick, use this." Finn tossed a greasy fast-food bag into the back seat. The smell of old French fries added to my nausea.

"Let us out, now." My voice rose with panic. "Zoe, please, please trust me. I forgive you for the sleepover. We have to get out."

Zoe turned to look at me. "What's going on?"

"Just get out. Now."

Zoe's eyes widened, and she reached over and grabbed the door handle. Just as she did, the light turned green. Finn hit the gas. We screeched through the intersection and onto the ramp for the expressway.

"Stop the car!" I shouted.

Finn kept driving.

"Didn't you hear her? She's going to throw up!" Zoe wrestled with her door.

"You'll be fine," Finn muttered. "Now settle down." We were driving faster and faster. I saw the Brooklyn Bridge in the rearview mirror. Manhattan was getting farther away.

"Hey." Zoe grabbed Finn's arm. "Let us out."

"Shut up." Finn shook off Zoe's arm.

"He's going to hurt you!"

Zoe turned back to me. "How do you know?" Her eyes were wide with fear.

"Your friend's crazy," Finn growled. "I'm not going to hurt you. Just sit still. I need to make a slight detour."

"He's lying!"

"Let us out now!" Zoe screamed.

"Shut up, both of you!" Finn grabbed her by the arm and shook her hard. "You, shut up, and make your friend do the same, okay?"

Zoe nodded. Up ahead I saw the exit for the Aqueduct. Finn was driving fast, one hand on the wheel, the other still gripping Zoe's arm.

Right before the exit, Finn took his hand off Zoe's arm. She turned and looked at me in the back seat. *Do something*, I mouthed. As she turned toward the front, she reached up and touched her mole. Finn took the exit without slowing down, the tires skidding as the car veered across the lanes. Up ahead I saw a four-way stop coming up fast. Too fast. I shut my eyes. The car flew through the intersection, jumped the curb, and slammed into the stop sign.

A stripe of pain shot across my shoulder before my seat belt catapulted me back against the seat. I heard the crunch of glass breaking and the whine of steel bending. Through the windshield, I watched the stop sign ricochet backward, flex for a moment, and then shiver, as if deciding what to do next.

Then, slowly, slowly, it fell forward, like a tree bending under the wind.

The sign stopped just above the windshield and hovered there, swaying up and down.

Everything was quiet.

Finn was slumped over the steering wheel. From below his hairline, a thin trickle of blood ran down the side of his face.

I was still holding the fast-food bag. I got it open just in time. When I was finished throwing up, I put the bag on the floor. We sat in silence for another minute.

"Is he okay?" I finally asked.

Zoe reached over and poked Finn. He groaned but didn't move. "What should we do?"

"Call the cops, I guess." Her voice was slow and flat, like her mind was a million miles away.

"Are *you* okay?"

Zoe shook her head slowly, as though just realizing she had been in the crash, too. She pressed her hands against her cheeks. Bits of glass sparkled in her hair. "I think so," she said in that same flat voice. Then, like she was just remembering I was in the car with her, she added, "You?"

"I think so." I released my seat belt.

We got out of the car and stood by the driver's side, watching Finn. He was breathing, but other than that not moving, his head against the steering wheel, eyes closed. Blood dripped from the bottom of the steering wheel in slow, fat drops. Zoe pulled her sleeve down over her hand, reached in the window, and found Finn's phone in his jacket pocket. She dialed 911, then put the phone in his lap. She turned to me. Her eyes were glassy, like she was looking straight through me. "Let's go," she said dully.

"Wait." I pulled my own sleeve down like she had, covering my fingers, then opened his door. "I just need to check something." I gingerly pinched the tail of his shirt between two fingers and pulled it up past the top of his jeans. I saw the leather handle and a glint of silver blade beneath the gap in his waistband.

I dropped his shirt and shut the door. "Let's go."

CHAPTER THIRTY-ONE

We walked in silence. The rain had stopped, and a thick fog made it impossible to see beyond the end of the block. I hoped we were heading west, in the direction of Manhattan. The tips of my fingers and tops of my ears felt cold, but my heart was racing, and my neck and chest were sweaty and hot.

"How did you do that?" I asked finally, not looking at Zoe.

"How did I do what?" She wasn't looking at me either, and her voice was still vague.

"Make Finn crash the car."

"I reached over and pushed the wheel," she said. "He must've been too drunk to react before we hit the stop sign."

"You pushed the wheel," I repeated slowly. "With your hand."

"Yes," Zoe said flatly. "I pushed the wheel with my hand."

"Not your mind."

Her expression changed, her eyes snapping into focus. "Oh, Tess, did you hit your head? Let me look and see if you're bleeding." Her voice sounded like her again.

I touched my head. I didn't remember hitting it. But I also didn't remember seeing Zoe push the wheel. I remembered her touching her mole—just the way she touched her mole right before the race—and right after that, the car flying through the intersection.

Just seconds before I had been positive she'd used her mind to make Finn crash the car.

Positive she'd made me win the race.

Positive she had a gift, like me.

Didn't she?

"You pushed the wheel with your hand, and that's what made him crash the car?" I repeated, giving my streak a gentle tug to clear my head. Out loud, it sounded a hell of a lot more plausible than the alternative. But I still wasn't sure I believed it.

"Yes! I pushed the wheel with my hand!" Zoe shouted, her voice now tinged with panic. Was she convincing me or herself? "Now can you please stop saying that? Oh my God, do you realize what just happened? This is so fucked up. I had no idea he wasn't wearing his seat belt. He could've gone through the windshield."

"He had a knife, Zoe," I said quietly.

"What? How do you know?" Her eyes were wild.

"I saw it under his shirt at the party," I said, not wanting to freak her out any more. But that wasn't the way it had happened. Or was it? Had I glimpsed the knife before we'd gotten in the car, and was that why I'd had the vision? Had Zoe made the car crash with her mind or with her hand? I didn't know what to believe anymore.

Zoe started to cry. "Oh my God, oh my God, oh my God, this can't be happening," she moaned.

"You saved yourself and me, too, probably. You did the right thing."

"The right thing? He was hurt bad, Tess. What if the cops find out we were in the car? Oh my God." She sank down on the side of the curb, wrapped her hands around her knees, and started rocking back and forth, sobbing. She was heading for a full-on panic attack. I needed to get us out of there.

"Zoe. Get up. We need to get as far away from here as possible," I said, hoping I sounded more confident than I felt.

Zoe started rocking faster.

"It's okay. No one will ever know about this. Let's just get home." I grabbed her arm and tugged, trying to pull her up, but the effort shot a bolt of pain across my shoulder, where I'd been thrown against the seat belt.

I gave up and sat on the curb next to her, tentatively touching the sore spot on my shoulder. I'd have a bruise in the morning.

"I can't believe this is happening," she groaned. "What if someone finds out? What if I go to jail? Or it goes on my record? I'll never get into college. I'll have no friends. Jake will break up with me. I'll become a total outcast, like . . ." she trailed off.

"Like me?" I finished for her.

"Sorry." She turned to look at me. "But it doesn't matter for you. Not the way it matters for me."

It was a horrible thing for her to say, but I knew what she meant. No one cared about me, not the way they cared about her. I didn't have a boyfriend, or friends, or a reputation to protect. Everyone already hated me. I wished I could take comfort in the fact, but I was scared as hell.

Was I truly losing my mind, thinking that not only I had powers but other people did, too?

Without even knowing it, had I already gone insane?

Eventually Zoe stopped rocking and wiped the tears off her face. She turned and looked at me for a moment, considering. "How did you know he was going to use the knife to hurt me?" she asked.

I hesitated. Maybe if I said I'd seen it happen in a vision, she'd admit that she had powers, too, that she'd used her mind, not her hand, to crash the car.

Maybe we'd even bond over our special abilities, become some crime-fighting superhero duo, Nightmare Girl and Miss Telekinesis.

I wanted it so badly, to know I wasn't alone.

But what if I told her about my dreams and she still insisted she'd pushed the wheel with her hand?

She'd definitely think I was crazy.

And I'd know I was.

"I wasn't positive," I said finally. "He just seemed so creepy, and when he started going away from Manhattan on the freeway I figured he wasn't taking us home."

Zoe nodded quickly, like the matter was settled, like I'd said what she wanted to hear. She pushed herself to her feet and held out her hand to me. "Well, thanks, I guess. You're probably right—he probably got exactly what he deserved. Sorry I got so upset."

"It's okay." I let her pull me up, careful to keep my shoulder still. "So what do we do about what happened?"

"Nothing! Have you not been listening to me? We can't tell anyone about this, okay?"

"Who would I tell? My only friend is dead."

She put her hands on my shoulders and turned me to face her. "I'm serious, Tess. You have to promise you won't tell, okay?"

"Promise."

We walked another block in silence. I could just make out the lights of the Brooklyn Bridge, far in the distance. I knew once we got back to Manhattan, back to our ordinary, daylight lives, she'd never admit to having magic powers. It was now or never.

"Can I ask you something?" I said. I wrapped my streak around my finger, then let it go. "Sometimes, before any of this, I used to see you looking at me, like at school and at practice. Is it just because you felt bad about the way Amanda treats me, or is there something else?"

Zoe sucked in her lower lip. "I did feel bad," she said slowly, "but I guess I was also curious about you. The way you're so different from everyone else."

I nodded, waiting for her to say more. When she was quiet for a few moments, I tried again. "Do you really think I set a new record for the course at the race today?"

She started to touch her mole, then dropped her hand. "How would I know?"

"You just said earlier . . ."

She hesitated. I could tell she was thinking about something, something that made her even more scared than what had happened with Finn and the car. But just then we heard the siren of a police car. It was far in the distance, but we both froze.

Her expression shifted. "Yeah," she said. "You were really fast."

The bridge was getting closer. Soon we'd be close enough to take the subway or find a taxi. I wasn't sure what the night meant. I felt like so much had changed, but maybe nothing had. Tabitha was still dead. My mom was still sick. Zoe was still queen of the Carolines.

I was still a freak.

And more alone than ever.

CHAPTER THIRTY-TWO

After the crash I basically stopped sleeping, relying on naps on my desk at school and iced double espressos to keep me going. Whenever I saw Zoe at school, she was glued to the side of Jake or Amanda, like she was afraid to be alone.

I would have surrounded myself with friends, too, if I'd had them.

I was too tired to show up for track practice, and when Coach stopped me in the hall and said he was replacing me with an alternate for the rest of the season, I just shrugged, unable to summon the energy to care.

My mom wasn't sleeping either. At night I'd hear her rustling around in the living room while I prowled the confines of my bedroom. We were like two rats in adjacent cages, rattling against our wire bars.

In the mornings we leaned against appliances in the kitchen— my mom propped against the stove, me slumped against the fridge, blinking and squinting in the overhead light while my dad tried to cajole my mom into eating something, convince me to get ready for school, and get himself out the door for work.

I couldn't remember a time when my mom had been this bad. She was losing weight, and the skin under her eyes was soft and wrinkly and mouse gray. She smelled terrible, like pee and dirty laundry. Ropes of hair hung lank around her face, the back tangled into one big knot. I was afraid that if I touched her she'd crumble into a pile of ash.

My dad was looking bad, too. He stopped pretending to make sure I ate dinner, just slumped on the sofa next to me when he got home from work at night, and we'd pass a bag of chips or pretzels back and forth, trying not to listen to the restless thumps coming from the bedroom. He didn't even have the heart to make fun of my TV shows.

Finally one night he came into my room and said my mom had agreed to check herself into the hospital. She'd gone once before, in the first year she was sick, and I knew this meant things were bad. It meant that she'd become a danger to herself, that being with us wasn't safe for her anymore.

I didn't have the energy to feel worried. I barely had the energy to care. I wished I could go with her, go someplace where they'd give me medicine so I could sleep and sleep and see nothing but blackness, see nothing at all.

• • •

The next day, Ms. Labos called me into her office during fifth period. Katie and Tabitha's dad were sitting on the sofa. Katie was wearing real sweatpants, not fancy workout gear, and a T-shirt with a stain on it. Her eyes were small and dull.

Tabitha's dad was wearing a suit. It looked too big for him in the shoulders and too short in the sleeves. I'd only met Mike once before, when he'd taken Tabitha and me out for ice cream on her thirteenth birthday, and I was surprised by how old he looked—so much older than I remembered. His hands were on his knees, and he sat staring at them, like they were animals that had crawled into his lap of their own accord.

When Katie saw me, she blinked at me for a minute, like my face was familiar but she couldn't remember my name. There was something about her expression that I recognized. Then, slowly, she got to her feet like her body weighed a million pounds and fell into me and gave me a big hug.

"Tesser," she whispered. "Hi, baby."

"Hi, Katie." When she didn't let go after a few seconds, I hugged her back. We stood that way long past the point of awkwardness, with Ms. Labos watching us and Tabitha's dad still sitting on the sofa, studying his hands.

Katie started to cry, snuffling against my shoulder. Tabitha's dad grimaced, then exhaled. Katie's chest heaved against mine.

"I'm sorry I haven't been in touch," I said. "I should've called but I lost my phone."

"No, no, I'm sorry I didn't reach out to *you*," Katie said. "This must be so awful for you. You must feel so alone." Katie had stopped hugging me by now and was staring into my eyes with a dreamy expression.

"Yeah, I guess."

Ms. Labos handed Katie some tissue and then handed me some, too, even though I wasn't crying. They both watched me, like they were waiting for me to burst into tears.

I blew my nose, just to do something with the tissue. "Maybe I'm still in shock?"

Katie looked at me sharply then, and for a second the fog cleared and I could see through to her heart, and it was like looking in the windows of an abandoned house. But then the fog descended again and she went all dreamy-eyed and I realized who she was acting like—my mom, on her strongest meds.

"Have a seat, Tess," Ms. Labos said, dragging over a chair from behind her desk. She was wearing a dark suit, even more shapeless than usual—possibly some type of mourning outfit. When she sat, the skirt rode up, revealing a run in her pantyhose just above the knee.

We all were quiet for a minute. "Katie and Mike—I mean, Mr. and Mrs. Smiley—I mean, you aren't Mrs. Smiley anymore, are you?" She blinked awkwardly at Katie, but Katie just stared at her. "I mean, Tabitha's parents and I wanted to talk to you about the initial results of the autopsy."

At the word *autopsy*, Tabitha's dad shifted his chair, raising one butt cheek, then settling back down.

"Like I said before, it will be a while before we get the full toxicology report, but we do have some preliminary findings from the blood work. According to the coroner, Tabitha's blood alcohol level was point two," Ms. Labos said, reading from the notes in her lap. "Which means she'd had a lot to drink that night." She looked up, blinked, then looked at the report again, like she couldn't believe she'd read right. "Like, *a lot*, a lot. Wow."

"Tabby wasn't a drinker," Katie said to Ms. Labos, ignoring me. "I mean, sure, all the popular kids drink, it goes along with partying, having fun, blowing off steam." She was bright-eyed again, as though remembering Tabitha as being one of the "popular kids" had revived her. "But she knew how to be careful. How to get a buzz without getting wasted."

Out of the corner of my eye I detected Mike shaking his head slightly, like he didn't think it was appropriate for his daughter to be getting wasted *or* buzzed, but when I glanced at him, he was looking out the window. His legs were crossed high, and he had his hands cupped tight over the top knee. His knuckles were white.

"Tess?" Ms. Labos said.

"Yeah?"

"Is that right? Was it usual for Tabitha to drink that much?"

I looked at Katie. "No. I mean, not that I knew of."

"But you knew she drank?"

"Ummm?" I remembered the New Year's Eve we'd mixed all the alcohols in the liquor cabinet, how she'd cried and said I was the best friend anyone could ever have and made me swear we'd be best friends forever, right before she opened my backpack, leaned over, and threw up in it. "I guess so?"

"What about the night she, uh, passed away?" Ms. Labos said, dropping her voice and shooting a quick glance at Mike. We all sucked in our breaths at "passed away," and I was actually glad she hadn't come right out and said "died."

"I don't know. I wasn't there. Why don't you ask Amanda? It was her party, right?"

Ms. Labos looked at Katie.

"Amanda says they weren't drinking," Katie said primly. "She says they had pizza and soda at Zoe's house, then snuck into the pool."

Sneaked, I corrected automatically in my head.

Ms. Labos saw me wince. "Tess?"

"Pizza and *soda?*" Even I knew how unlikely that sounded.

"Amanda is completely destroyed by what happened. I don't see why she'd lie." Katie glowed again for a moment. She'd always been involved in the social structure of the school—too involved, if you ask me—and she knew how powerful Amanda was.

"But what about before? Is it possible Tabitha was drinking on her own, before she went to Zoe's house?" Ms. Labos asked.

"You know, pregaming?" Katie chimed in. Ms. Labos gave a worried smile and nod.

"I have no idea."

"You talked to her for five minutes that night," Katie said.

"Who told you that?" I sounded more defensive than I'd meant.

"Tabitha's phone was ruined in the pool," Ms. Labos said, looking at her notes again. "But the phone company gave us records of her incoming and outgoing calls."

"You were the last person she talked to," Mike said. It was the first time he'd spoken, and we all jumped, then pretended like it hadn't happened, like when someone burps out loud.

"Oh," I said softly. I sat on my hand to keep myself from reaching for my streak again. Remembering the things I'd said to her on the phone made me feel sick. "She didn't sound drunk when I talked to her. I think she was actually drinking a peppermint tea."

"But did she say anything about planning to drink that night? Before she met the other girls?"

That didn't sound like Tabitha, but then, how well had I actually known her?

Was Tabitha a secret drinker? Was the key to her acceptance by the popular girls the fact that she was completely wasted every time she hung out with them? It was hard to believe. But I definitely didn't believe that Amanda's party had consisted of pin the tail on the donkey and musical chairs.

"Or something else? Some sort of drugs?" Ms. Labos added. "Something that might have interacted with the alcohol?"

Amanda had warned Nikki at the sleepover not to say anything about drinking or drugs. "You should talk to Amanda and those guys. They're the ones she was hanging out with before she . . . passed away."

Katie turned to me so quickly I swear I heard the air move around her. Her eyes were suddenly focused and filled with rage. "We did talk to Amanda. She said Tabitha was acting weird that night. She said she wasn't sure if she'd been drinking, but she was definitely upset. And she said she thought it had to do with you."

"With me?"

"You told me you and Tabitha had had a fight, remember, Tess?" Ms. Labos said. "Is it possible she was upset you weren't friends anymore?"

"It's not like that at all. She was the one who dropped me."
Mike frowned. "Why?"
We all looked at him again. I took a breath. "She wanted to be popular." It sounded pathetic.

"And you couldn't stay friends because of that?" He looked genuinely confused.

"That's what we were talking about that night. I wanted to still be friends. Tabitha said it was impossible."

"That's not true!" Katie burst out. "Tabby wasn't like that. She wouldn't drop someone just because they were less popular than she was. She told me you were the one who didn't want to be friends anymore."

Katie started crying again and covered her face with her hands. Mike went back to looking out the window.

Ms. Labos took a deep, shaky breath. She pulled her skirt down over her potato-shaped knees, then folded her hands in her lap in an imitation of someone creating order out of chaos. "Maybe you can just tell us exactly what you said to Tabitha that night on the phone."

That she was a lobotomized puppet. That she was pathetic. That I'd rather be a loser freak than be like her.

And then I had a vision of her death, and I didn't do anything to stop it.

I let her die.

"I don't remember," I mumbled.

Katie wiped her face with the heels of her palms hard enough to leave red streaks across her cheeks for a second. She stood up and brushed her hands on her sweatpants, then took a pair of sunglasses from her bag and shoved them on her face.

"Okay, Tess," she said. "If that's all you want to say now, that's fine. But sooner or later you're going to have to tell the truth."

"Jesus, Katherine, leave the girl alone." Mike was on his feet, his face red, his fists clenched at his sides. "She wasn't even there. It's not her fault."

Tabitha had said he had a temper. I hated to imagine what it would feel like to have that rage directed at me, how mad he'd be if he found out how wrong he was.

CHAPTER THIRTY-THREE

By lunchtime the next day, the story had spread so widely across school even I'd heard it: Tabitha and I had had a fight because I was jealous that she was popular and I wasn't. I'd said horrible things to her, and she'd gone off and finished an entire bottle of peach schnapps (or vanilla vodka or Baileys Irish Cream, depending on who was telling the story) by herself. When she showed up at Amanda's party, she was acting crazy, but everyone knew she was a spaz, so no one realized how drunk she was. They went to the pool, she fell in, hit her head, and died.

Because of me.

If people had ignored me before, now they looked downright afraid of me. The crowds parted when I walked down the hall, like even accidental contact with me could be fatal.

Was the story true? I didn't even know anymore.

I put a note in Zoe's locker, telling her to meet me in the alley behind school after the last bell. After final period, I put my sweatshirt hood up and walked out of school as fast as I could.

The alley was dirty and dark, with broken bottles and crumbling bricks. It was where kids went to get high, but today it was deserted. I leaned against a wall, not caring if my sweatshirt got soot on it.

I tilted my head back and looked up at the sky. It was a gray day, the clouds already knitting together in the beginning of dusk. In two weeks it would be Halloween.

Tabitha had loved Halloween. She always dressed up like Daphne from Scooby-Doo, which left me to be Velma, and we handed out candy to all the little kids in her building, then watched movies and made ourselves sick on fun-sized Snickers.

Not this year.

If she hadn't died, she'd probably be planning to go to some party, where she'd dress up like a sexy cat or sexy baby, then go ironically trick-or-treating.

How long would Amanda and the rest have let her hang around them? I thought about Amanda, how much different everything would be if she'd been the one to hit her head in the pool instead of Tabitha.

"So, are you going to tell me where you've been?"

Zoe was walking toward me, picking her way across the loose gravel in her high-heeled boots.

"What do you mean? I've been right here, waiting for you."

"No, I mean since that night. You've been avoiding me."

"I thought you were avoiding me."

"Whatever." She sounded annoyed. "I've been texting you. The cops came to my house."

"About Tabitha?"

"About Finn. The paramedics found my number in his phone."

"Oh my God," I said. "You said you were going to give him a fake number."

She shrugged and waved her hand, like she was pushing smoke out of her face.

"What did you tell the cops?"

"I said he gave us a ride to the subway, but we weren't in the car when he crashed. I guess he was freaked out enough by what happened that he said basically the same thing."

"So he's okay?"

"He broke a bunch of ribs, but he'll live." She sounded as cold and uncaring as the night of her slumber party, when she'd said she didn't want me at her house.

A breeze blew down the alley, stirring up soot and lifting an old plastic bag. It caught against my ankle before skittering away. I rubbed my arms, suddenly chilled.

"Sorry you had to do that by yourself."

Zoe shrugged. "Cops are stupid." I could picture it, Zoe going all big-eyed and quiet-voiced, acting shocked when they told her what had happened to the nice man who'd given us a ride after the party. Had she acted the same way when she'd talked to them after Tabitha died?

"Are you okay otherwise?" I said. "I mean, about that night."

"I don't know." She looked at the ground and kicked a piece of concrete. She exhaled. "Mostly I try not to think about it."

"Me, too."

She kept kicking the ground, then looked up at me. "Have you told anyone about what happened?"

"Of course not." One of the chunks of rubble landed near me, and I kicked it back toward her. "Did you tell anyone?"

"Of course not."

"Not even Amanda?"

She shook her head, not meeting my eyes. I knew she wouldn't tell me if she had.

"Not even Jake?" I couldn't help myself.

She looked straight at me and laughed. "No. No way."

"Oh." Then, fighting to keep the hope out of my voice, I added, "You didn't break up, did you?"

"Not even close." She narrowed her eyes. "Sorry."

"What?" I tried to look like I had no idea what she was talking about. "I just thought, you were so mad at him that night when he kept texting you . . ."

Zoe sighed and flipped her hair to the other side, and in that moment the sun came out from behind a cloud and hit her face and she looked as beautiful and perfect as ever. "We'll never break up. I mean, not until we go to college. And then we'll probably go through this awkward few months where we're broken up but whenever we're home we have sex and get all depressed, and then eventually we'll stop even doing that and maybe then we'll be friends for real. Right now it's like he's my boyfriend, but he's not even my friend. We're just so used to each other, it's hard for us to imagine life without the other one, but I don't know if we'd be together if we met today."

Just like Tabitha and me, before she decided to become popular, minus the sex part. But I didn't say that. Instead, I said, "Wow."

"Yeah." Zoe shook her head sadly. "I just feel like so many people depend on us to be together. Like everyone would be disappointed if we broke up. We're like this . . ."

". . . golden couple," I finished the quote.

"Exactly. Like Caroline and Jake in *Sixteen Candles*."

I didn't point out that Caroline and Jake break up at the end of *Sixteen Candles*. But Zoe must've realized it, because she looked around the alley, like she'd just noticed where we were. "Anyway, I don't know why I'm telling you all this. What are we doing back here?"

"You have to tell me what happened the night Tabitha died." I snapped out of my reverie about Jake and *Sixteen Candles* and remembered how screwed-up real life was.

"You already know. The whole school knows. She dove into the pool, hit her head, and drowned."

"The whole school thinks it's my fault."

Zoe shrugged impatiently. "Fuck the whole school."

"Easy for you to say. And it's not just the other kids. Tabitha's parents think so, too."

"Her parents?" Now Zoe was paying attention.

"Apparently her blood alcohol was super high. Were you drinking?"

Zoe bugged her eyes at me. "Duh."

"Is that why Amanda is lying about what happened? 'Cause she's worried you'll get in trouble if the cops find out you were drinking at the pool?"

"What makes you think Amanda's lying?"

"Because I got called into Ms. Labos's office, where Tabitha's parents basically accused me of killing their daughter."

Zoe sucked in her breath. "You didn't tell them anything, did you?"

"I don't have anything *to* tell them."

"Exactly."

We were quiet for a moment. An ambulance roared down the street at the end of the alley, its siren reverberating off the walls of the buildings around us. Zoe took her phone out of her pocket, then put it back without looking at it. All of a sudden she smiled, her get-anything-from-anyone smile. "Don't worry about Amanda, okay? Tabitha's parents are just looking for someone to blame, and Ms. Labos is probably worried about the school being sued. What happened to Tabitha was an accident. A tragic accident."

"Right," I said slowly. "A tragic accident."

• • •

It wasn't until I was lying in bed that night, wrapping and unwrapping my finger in my streak, that I remembered Zoe's words: *a tragic accident.* It was exactly what Amanda had told Nikki to say if the cops asked her any questions. Tabitha's death was a tragic accident.

Except I knew, without understanding how I knew, that it hadn't been an accident at all.

CHAPTER THIRTY-FOUR

Mike and Katie rented a movie theater for a memorial for Tabitha. The day of the memorial, all the popular girls wore black to school, and each carried a single yellow rose. Amanda clutched a yellow handkerchief in her other hand and kept dabbing at her eyes with it and sniffing loudly during class. After dismissal, school buses drove us to the theater.

No one sat next to me.

As the theater filled, kids whispered and giggled and threw pens at each other, like any other field trip. Then the popular girls walked in, staring straight ahead, looking super serious and important, and everyone quieted down.

Amanda stopped at Katie and Mike's row in the front and grabbed both of Katie's hands and started shaking with sobs. Zoe stood behind her. She was holding her rose awkwardly, like it was a flier someone had handed her that she didn't know what to do with. That sparkly glow she normally had was gone. I couldn't help but think even she knew Amanda was being over the top.

Katie went up on the stage in front of the curtain and adjusted the microphone. She looked better than she'd looked in Ms. Labos's office—she was wearing makeup and a black wrap dress with yellow stripes that made her look like an anorexic bumblebee.

The curtain opened, and the lights went down, and pictures of Tabitha started flashing on the movie screen.

As an orchestral version of "Tears in Heaven" played, a larger-than-life Tabitha aged from chubby, frizzy-haired toddler to chubby, frizzy-haired tween. In nearly every picture, she had a smudge of something on her face, or her shirt was misbuttoned, or her belly was sticking out, but in every single picture she was grinning as wide as she could, and in several she had her arms thrown open, as though to show the world how truly, desperately happy she was.

As the slide show played, Katie talked about how popular Tabitha had always been, how much she had loved Whitman, and what a great community she'd found in the school.

All lies.

She didn't mention me once. She'd even made sure to not include any pictures that had me in them.

Katie used to call me "Tesser." She used to give me her old workout clothes, because there was no way they'd fit Tabitha. It wasn't like I was going to be prancing around in a sweatshirt that said *Juicy!* across my nonexistent chest, but I'd always pretended to be grateful.

Sometimes I'd thought maybe Katie secretly wished Tabitha were more like me—even though I was an outcast freak, I was quiet, and thin, and too self-conscious to do anything that would truly embarrass her.

Probably she thought I secretly wished my mom were more like her, too. Maybe I had, but now, sitting in the theater at Tabitha's memorial, I realized how wrong I'd been.

• • •

The slide show ended with a picture of Tabitha that must have been taken right before she died, because her hair was straight and shiny, and she looked skinny and orange. She was smiling a small, tentative, close-mouthed smile, a smile I'd never seen before. It belonged to a Tabitha I didn't recognize, a Tabitha I hadn't even been friends with. She was standing next to Katie, and Katie had her arm around Tabitha's shoulder, and I realized it was the only picture where Tabitha hadn't been alone. I tried to remember another time Katie had let herself be photographed with her daughter, but I couldn't.

Katie finished by saying her only comfort was that Tabitha had left the world surrounded by such good friends. Then all the popular girls went up on stage, clutching their roses, and sang "You'll Never Walk Alone." Did any of them know that Tabitha had wanted to be in the school production of *Carousel* but hadn't even been cast in the chorus?

Amanda kept wiping her eyes as they sang and leaning on Imani, who was standing next to her. Zoe looked straight ahead. I couldn't tell if she was singing or just mouthing the words.

When they were done with the song, each girl came forward, one by one, said, "Goodbye, Tabitha," and dropped her rose in a pile at the edge of the stage.

When it was Amanda's turn, she said, "Goodbye, Tabitha," then turned toward the crowd. "Your real friends will never forget you."

I could feel the kids sitting near me staring at me. I couldn't take it anymore.

I got up and ran.

I hid in a stall in the bathroom, my feet pulled up on the seat, trying not to make a sound. Girls came in and out of the bathroom, some sniffling, others laughing.

I held my breath, willing my heart to stop beating so wildly. I waited until the door stopped opening and closing, until I heard no sounds from the lobby, until I was sure all the buses had left to go back to school. Then I counted to two hundred, just to be safe.

I came out of the stall.

Katie was standing against the door, her arms folded across her chest.

"Oh!" I said. "I didn't know anyone was in here."

"I was waiting for you," Katie said.

I went to the sink and started washing my hands. "That was a lovely, uh, service," I said awkwardly. "Tabitha would've loved it."

Katie nodded distractedly. She walked over next to me and leaned forward, examining her face in the mirror. Up close, I could see how thick her makeup was. The skin on her neck where she wasn't wearing foundation looked yellow, and the veins stood out like cords. She'd always been skinny, but she'd lost even more weight since Tabitha died. She reached up and touched her lips.

"Things got intense in Heather's office the other day," she said. It took me a moment to remember Heather was Ms. Labos. "I hope you didn't feel like you were being interrogated."

I heard Zoe's words in my mind: *a tragic accident, a tragic accident.*

"I just wish I could help you more." I instinctively reached for my streak, then tried to make the gesture look like I was smoothing my hair in the mirror.

"Me, too." Katie kept her eyes on the mirror. She rummaged in her bag and pulled out a pair of sunglasses and started to put them on, then stopped and turned to me. "Please, if you cared about Tabitha at all—if you care about me at all—please just tell me what happened that night. It's just the two of us now. I've been a second mother to you. I deserve the truth."

I recognized her tone—it was the *we're all best girlfriends* tone she'd use when she wanted Tabitha and me to gossip with her about the popular girls.

A tragic accident. A tragic accident.

"Honestly, Katie, I told you the truth."

"Are you sure there's nothing you're leaving out? You swear that phone call was the last time you talked to her?"

I had a flash of my dream, my mom on the sofa, rubbing my feet. Katie looked so desperate and so sad. "Not exactly," I admitted.

"Then what, exactly?"

"I texted her. I felt bad about the way our phone call ended and I couldn't sleep, so I texted her, asking if we could talk."

Katie exhaled, like she'd been waiting for me to admit this. "And then?"

"Then nothing. She didn't text back. I fell asleep. The next morning my dad told me she'd . . . told me what happened."

"Why didn't you tell us this the other day?"

"Because I didn't think it mattered. Like I said, I never heard back from her."

Katie stared at me for a long moment. Her shoulders slumped. "Oh, Tess. I wish so bad I could believe you. It's just . . . let me see your phone." She held out her hand.

"I lost it. I told you in Ms. Labos's office, remember?"

She made a baffled expression, like why would I expect her to remember something as inconsequential as the whereabouts of my phone. "When did you lose it?"

"The night Tabitha died." I realized how suspicious it sounded. I'd looked behind the sofa, under the sofa, in the cushions of the sofa, and everywhere in my room, but our apartment was a black hole in that way. The phone could be anywhere. It would turn up eventually—stuff always did—but I could see Katie wasn't interested in *eventually*.

"Tess, I know you saw Tabitha the night she died," Katie said with a heavy sigh, pushing the sunglasses onto her face and turning back to the mirror.

"What are you talking about?"

"Amanda told us what happened."

"Amanda?"

"She says you texted Tabitha that night, like you said. But she also says you told her to come meet you. You wouldn't take no for an answer, so she left the pool and met you outside. And when she came back, she was acting very weird. And then she dove into the pool . . ."

"What? That's not true!" My voice came out choked with panic.

"Why would Amanda say that then?"

"Because she hates me. Because they were all drinking, and she doesn't want to get in trouble. I don't know," I admitted. "But you can't believe Amanda."

"She's not the only one who says Tabitha met you."

"Who else?"

"Zoe."

CHAPTER THIRTY-FIVE

I was up most of the night trying to figure out why Zoe would have told Katie I met Tabitha outside the night she died, but finally I fell into a twitchy, half-lucid sleep just before dawn, no closer to answers than when I'd gone to bed. I woke up a few hours later with my dad sitting on the edge of my bed, and for a second I panicked that he was going to tell me someone else had died. But he just said there were bagels and coffee in the kitchen and it was a beautiful Saturday and I shouldn't waste it sleeping. He waited until I'd had a cup of coffee and was spreading olive cream cheese on my bagel to say that he was going to visit my mom, and he hoped I'd come, too.

I hadn't gone to see my mom since she'd checked herself into the hospital. The secret truth was, with everything that was happening at school, I hadn't even thought about her that much.

The even more secret truth was it had been a relief not having her around to worry about, on top of everything else.

My dad looked down at his bagel, which he hadn't even taken a bite of yet, waiting for me to answer. His eyes looked so tired. I knew I looked like hell, too. The last thing I wanted was to go to the hospital and see how terrible my mom looked, completing the portrait of our falling-apart family, each of us in our own little world of misery.

"Sure," I said, "let me just take a shower."

• • •

At the hospital we took the elevator to the eighth floor, and my dad buzzed the intercom. Through the window of the door I could see the nurses at their station. One of them looked up and saw my dad and buzzed us in. I guess he must've been there a lot for them to recognize him.

There was a big thing of hand sanitizer on a stand right by the door. It seemed funny, like you could catch whatever the people in the crazy ward had from touching them. Or you could infect them with your sanity. Assuming you were sane going in. Maybe once the doctors saw me, they'd say I had to stay, too.

Maybe they'd be right.

My mom was sitting on a twin bed in her room. She was wearing sweatpants, my dad's Penn sweatshirt, and slippers. Her hair was in a ponytail. I was surprised to see how much better she looked than the last time I'd seen her—cleaner, and not as tired.

She got up and gave me a hug, and it was the same as always—too hard, so I couldn't breathe, but nice, in a way, the kind of pain you want to make yourself hold still for. "Hello, my magical, magical girl," she whispered into my hair.

She smelled like her lotion and medicine and something else, something familiar I couldn't place.

After she finished hugging me, she hugged my dad and I looked around her room. There was another twin bed opposite hers and two dressers. Her contact lens stuff was on top of one of the dressers.

There was an ugly painting of seagulls flying over the ocean on the wall. It looked glued to the wall, like in a hotel. Maybe patients tried to steal the art, or maybe they bashed each other over the head with it.

We all went to the common room. It had worn armchairs and drab carpet and a water cooler in the corner with a dispenser with little paper cone cups. Like her room, there was nothing there to indicate this was a facility for crazy people. No straitjackets hanging from the walls. No candy dispensers full of Prozac. It was more like what was missing that made it seem different. No magazines, no throw pillows, no lamps, no end tables. The overhead light was bright. Did it have a camera hidden inside, so the nurses could watch us from their station?

I let my dad do most of the talking, because I wasn't sure what to say to someone in the loony bin. The last time my mom had gone to the hospital, I had been too young to visit. Now I wished I'd come up with an excuse not to go this time. I kept reminding myself we were only here for a little while; I was a visitor, not a patient.

Not yet.

I could feel my dad shooting me little looks out of the corner of his eye, waiting for me to join in the conversation, but I worried if I said the wrong word, guards would come in and drag me away or drag my mom away, like how you get arrested if you say *bomb* at the airport.

I didn't know what the wrong word would be—crazy, maybe? Suicide? Insane asylum? I had the feeling we were all supposed to pretend we were someplace else, like a dentist's office or the world's most uninviting living room. There wasn't even a TV.

My dad prattled away, filling the silence with chitchat. The shower had been acting funny but he'd called the plumber; Juju had caught a cockroach and was very proud of himself; it was so cold last night the weatherman had predicted snow, but it was warmer this morning.

When he said this I realized my mom must not have gone outside since she'd been there. They held hands while he talked and she smiled vaguely and nodded, but I could tell she wasn't paying attention.

At least my mom had my dad to visit her. If I wound up in a place like this, would anyone come see me?

Then, like they'd agreed on it beforehand, my dad said in a very stagy way that he had a call to make and was going to go outside. As he left he gave me a look that meant I'd better talk to my mom while he was gone, or else. I tried not to show how panicked I felt as the door shut behind him.

My mom slowly turned to me, like she'd forgotten I was there. "How's everything been with you?"

Horrible. Unbearable. I'm so scared and confused. Please help me. "Fine. Good."

"What about track?"

Can't you see I'm so tired I can barely stand upright, let alone run a mile? "Fine."

We were both quiet. I was probably supposed to ask her how she was doing now, but I couldn't do it. I reached up and tugged on my streak until it hurt. "Are you coming home soon?"

"I hope so." She gave me a wilted smile and suddenly she looked tired again, like the restedness was just a layer of makeup on top of her exhausted skin. Anger bubbled in my stomach.

"Why don't you just come home, then?" It wasn't like I desperately wanted her at home. But I didn't want her in this place either.

"I'm not sure I'm ready." She stopped smiling. She looked at the wall as she spoke and shuffled one slipper lightly against the carpet. "My doctor thinks it might be good for me to stay a bit longer."

"How much longer?"

Shush shush shush went her slipper. I wanted to reach down and grab her foot and make her stop. "I don't know." She rubbed the back of her neck. "They're trying a new medication, and they want me to stay here in case there are any side effects."

"Oh." The medicine cabinet at home was filled with bottles of pills, none of which had worked. Was that why she was staying? Or did she just prefer the hospital to being at home with my dad and me?

I got up from the sofa and went over to look at a painting on the wall by the door. It was even uglier than the one in her room. Birds again, this time flying over sand dunes. Sort of an ironic subject for a mental hospital. "Why are all the paintings glued to the walls?"

My mom looked up slowly. "Are they? I hadn't noticed. I have no idea."

I did a tour of the perimeter of the room, keeping clear of the sofa. "How come no one else is in here?"

"Most of them are in the smoking room."

"Does everyone here smoke?"

"Pretty much." She nodded. Color rose in her cheeks. That was the familiar smell. Cigarettes.

"Have you started again?"

She looked down at her hands. "Just a few," she mumbled. "I'll stop again once I come home, I promise. It just helps in here."

In a way it was comforting to know she was back to sneaking cigarettes. It made her seem more like her old self. But it was also depressing. It meant nothing had changed.

I flopped back on the sofa. It was weird how quickly I was getting comfortable in that room, how easily it stopped seeming strange. Maybe I belonged there, too. Maybe after a few days I wouldn't want to leave either.

"Why is there no TV?" I asked, after a few moments of uncomfortable silence.

"It's in the smoking room, too."

"Do you want to go in there?" She could smoke, and I could do something other than sit there listening to my deafening inability to make conversation.

My mom shook her head, then reached up and touched her temple, like the sudden movement had been painful. "I want to talk to you. Tell me stuff about what's been going on."

She didn't even know about Tabitha's memorial service. Or about what Katie had said in Ms. Labos's office. Or anything that had happened since the night Tabitha died.

I remembered sitting on the sofa with her, the way she rubbed my feet—the way it hurt but felt good. I remembered her encouraging me to text Tabitha. Not encouraging. Insisting.

That was why I'd listened to her.

That was why I'd texted Tabitha.

Not because I'd thought it would make a difference for Tabitha.

Because I thought it would make a difference for my mom.

"Hey." I sat up suddenly. "You don't know what happened to my phone, do you?"

"Huh?" My mom had been staring at me dreamily, but when I sat up she gave a little shake, like her mind had been a million miles away.

"My phone. I can't find it. You haven't seen it, have you?"

She started making vague searching gestures around the sofa where we were sitting, patting at the cushions.

"No, not here. At home. I lost it the night Tabitha died."

She stared at me, and her lips parted a little, like she wanted to speak but couldn't make her mouth work right. Whatever drugs they were giving her must have been strong. She licked her lips and swallowed. "Your phone," she repeated.

I couldn't stand to see her like this, not for one more minute. It was hopeless. Everything was hopeless.

"Tess, I . . ." she started to say, then stopped. "Your phone . . ." she tried again.

She must've taken a dose of medication right before we'd arrived, and it was just hitting peak strength now. All the color was gone from her face, and she looked about to pass out. She started plucking at the threads in the sofa cover, as though my phone were hidden underneath.

"Never mind." She could barely remember my name. It was stupid to think she'd have any idea what had happened weeks ago.

"Tess, I'm sorry," she said, slurring her words. "My brain . . ." She put her hands on the side of her head. "I wish I could remember."

"Just forget it, okay?" I didn't want to hear any more.

"No, just give me a minute. You were asking me something important."

"Seriously, stop talking! You're just making things worse!" I pulled up my hood and turned away from her. Why did she even bother asking about me, when she obviously couldn't even take care of her own self? Why had my dad brought me here, when it wasn't doing either of us any good?

Just then the door opened and my dad walked in. I was sitting with my arms folded, not looking at my mom. My mom was sitting on the other end of the sofa, still plucking at the cover. She was crying softly, not even bothering to wipe her eyes.

"What happened?"

"Nothing. Can we just go?"

He looked at me, then looked at my mom. "Sylvie, what's wrong?" He turned to me. "What did you say to her?"

"Nothing!"

He was already sitting down next to her, putting his arms around her, turning his back to me.

"I'll wait in the hall." I slunk out the door. Once again, I was the bad guy. Once again, I'd made my mom sad. Once again, my dad had to rescue her. Everything was different, but nothing had changed at all.

CHAPTER THIRTY-SIX

As soon as we were back in the apartment, my dad went in his bedroom and shut the door. I scooped Jujube off the sofa and carried him into my room and got into bed and pulled him under the covers with me. I was squeezing him so tightly he let out a little yelp. When I let him go, he jumped out of the bed and ran to the door and started scratching.

"I'm sorry, buddy," I said. "Please come back and talk to me. Everyone hates me right now except you."

He didn't answer, just sat by the door with his back to me and his tail twitching, making a low moaning noise. Finally I got out of bed and let him out.

"You too, huh?" I said as he dashed out of the room.

I got back in bed and tried to fall asleep. All I wanted was a few hours of rest, a few hours of a different reality. I didn't even care if I had one of my dreams. It was starting to feel like nothing I imagined could be as bad as what I was living. But just as I started to drift off, I remembered what Katie had said the day of Tabitha's memorial.

Both Amanda and Zoe had said I'd met Tabitha outside the school the night she died.

They had to be lying.

Didn't they?

All I remembered was falling asleep on the sofa, and my dad waking me up the next morning and telling me Tabitha was dead.

Wasn't that what had happened?

I heard the sound of my mother's slipper shuffling against the carpet—*shush, shush, shush*. I had a flash of my own feet in the same slippers, moving in the same restless, agitated way, against the same floor.

For every problem there's a solution.

I threw off the covers and got out of bed. I really wished I could find my phone. My stomach felt full of acid and my legs were shaky.

The last time I had tried to talk to Zoe about the night Tabitha died, I'd gotten distracted when she started talking about Jake, and hadn't pushed her about exactly what "tragic accident" was supposed to mean.

Had she purposely changed the subject?

I shoved my feet in my shoes, grabbed my bag, and headed for the door.

"I'm going out, in case you care," I yelled toward my dad's closed door. I waited a second and when there was no answer, let myself out of the apartment.

CHAPTER THIRTY-SEVEN

I was so preoccupied thinking about how everyone in the world, including my cat, currently hated me, I didn't even notice there was someone sitting on the stoop outside Zoe's apartment building until I was halfway up the steps and the person said hi to me.

Or rather, the person said, "Hey, Tess."

And that's how I discovered Jake Boylan knew my name.

He was leaning back against the steps, resting on his elbows, looking at his phone. His body was a perfect study in angles. A basketball sat on the step next to him, and just by its proximity to him it looked like something more noble than a basketball, like something rare and precious.

I froze. What was I supposed to do? Pretend I didn't hear him? Act lost? Turn around and run?

I did the bravest, craziest thing I could imagine.

I said hi back.

Or rather, I said, "Hey, Jake."

"Looking for Zoe?" He slid the phone into the pocket of his jeans. His stomach looked hard and rippled under his T-shirt.

My thoughts slowed as I stared at the way his shirt draped across his ribcage. Just beneath the cotton was Jake's skin . . . warm, smooth skin that probably tasted like caramel, sweet and a little bit salty . . . I shook myself. Answer him, you idiot. "Do you know if she's home?" Like Jake would be just hanging out on her front steps if Zoe were home. Ugh.

"On her way. The trains are all messed up."

"Cool." Why was it cool that the trains were messed up? Ugh ugh ugh. I was still standing halfway up the steps. I had the feeling I might stay frozen there forever, staring at Jake's midsection until my leg muscles gave out and I tumbled down to the sidewalk.

If I looked directly at his face I would probably faint.

"Wanna wait with me?" He gestured to the step.

"Okay." I miraculously managed to lower my body next to his without falling on my head. We were sitting close enough that I could smell his scent—a combination of Speed Stick and dryer sheets, pine mixed with sweet. Closer than I'd ever been to him before. Closer than I'd ever thought I'd be.

I wished, more than anything, that Tabitha were still alive, so I could tell her about this.

She would've been so happy for me.

She really would've.

I missed her.

"So what's going on?"

"Huh?" I squinted at Jake. He was so gorgeous, it was like looking at the sun. Too dangerous to do with your eyes wide open.

"How is your weekend?" He spoke slowly, like he'd just remembered I might be mentally disabled.

"Ummm? Weird?"

"Why weird?"

"I went to visit my mom today. She's in the hospital." What was I doing? I'd spent most of my life trying to hide the fact that my mom was crazy, and now I'd just practically blurted it out to the boy I loved most in the world, the very first time I got a chance to speak to him. When I did stuff like this, I understood why everyone thought I was a freak.

Jake nodded. "I hate hospitals." He lifted the basketball with the palm of one hand. "I had to have ankle surgery once. It sucked." He bounced the ball lightly on the step between his feet.

"Yeah," I agreed. Probably it was best he hadn't asked what was wrong with my mom. "That does suck."

We were quiet for a minute except for the thump, thump, thump of the ball.

"Is it better now?"

"Huh?"

"Your ankle."

"Oh yeah. Good as new." He grabbed the ball, tossed it into the air above his head, caught it with one hand, then held out his foot, rotating his ankle proudly. "Better, actually. I snapped my Achilles tendon, and the way they reconnect the tendon, it makes it inherently stronger than before. I'll probably have to get the other one done at some point."

"Wow." Jake was . . . nice. This revelation didn't make him any less gorgeous, but it made it easier to look at him. So did the fact that he'd used "inherently" wrong. We were practically having a normal conversation, the kind where you look at the other person when he speaks and aren't so busy imagining what he looks like under his T-shirt you don't hear a word he says.

"You do track with Zoe, right?"

I nodded, vowing to rejoin the team as soon as possible. Not only did Jake know my name, he knew actual things about me. And was willing to be seen talking to me by anyone who happened to be passing by.

"How are your ankles?"

I looked down, considering my feet. I hadn't shaved my legs in a while, and a few prickly hairs were visible between the hem of my jeans and the tops of my Converse. I pulled my feet in against the step. "So far, so good."

"What about your knees?"

"They're okay, too. Knock on, uh, cartilage." I rapped on my knees with my knuckles. It was the kind of dorky joke my dad would make, and my face turned red as I heard myself say it. But Jake didn't seem to notice.

"Yeah," he said with a sigh. "I'm always telling Zoe she has to protect her joints. You can't take them for granted. But she never listens." He turned to me, an expression of mild outrage on his face. "Do you ever see her stretching at meets? She says stretching is boring. You know what's boring? Recovering from ankle surgery."

"You're totally right." You know what else was maybe the tiniest bit boring? This conversation. I banished the thought from my mind as soon as I had it. It felt like blasphemy even thinking Jake was less than amazing in any way.

Jake sat up, laced his fingers, and stretched his arms over his head, making an exaggerated yawning growl. His T-shirt pulled up, revealing a strip of skin at the waist. Definitely not boring. I tried not to stare. Was he doing it on purpose? How could he not know how incredible every inch of his body was, and what it did to a mortal girl like me to see even a few centimeters of it? He lowered his arms, pulled his phone out of his pocket, and glanced at the display. "Where is she?" he muttered.

With any luck, trapped under something heavy.

He grabbed the ball, jumped from the step to the sidewalk, and bounced the ball off the bottom step, saying, "Think fast." I caught the ball and bounced it back.

"So, no offense, but did you and Zoe have plans today?" He returned the ball, this time with enough topspin I had to reach for it. "'Cause I thought we did, and she didn't mention anything about you."

"No." I fumbled the ball. "I just wanted to talk to her. I lost my phone, and I needed to get out of the house anyway." Talking to Jake had successfully erased all memories of my dad, my mom, and every other unpleasant aspect of my real life, including the reason I had been so desperate to talk to Zoe.

Somewhere, deep in my brain, my desire for answers about what had happened at the pool ticked like a clock, but talking to Jake was like smothering that clock under many, many pillows. I shot the ball back to him.

"That's cool." He caught the ball one-handed. "It's good if you're friends with her. She needs to hang out with different people besides Amanda and those bitches." He dribbled a figure eight between his legs.

"Wait. You think Amanda's a bitch?"

"Amanda *is* a bitch." He faked shooting me the ball. "Why, don't you think she is?"

"No no no no, I *definitely* think Amanda Price is a bitch. I just didn't know her friends thought that, too."

"Is Zoe Amanda's friend?" He cocked his head. "I don't know. Girls are weird. I think Zoe knows Amanda's a bitch, too."

"Then why does she hang out with her?"

Jake shrugged. "Your guess is as good as mine. If I ask Zoe to do something, it's like she gets pleasure out of doing the exact opposite, but if Amanda asks her for something, she's incapable of saying no." A wisp of annoyance curled around his tone. I remembered his texts the night I met Zoe at the café—the growing desperation, irritation tinged with panic. Was that why he was being so nice to me? Did he want to make Zoe jealous, pay her back for ignoring him that night? As ridiculous as it was to think Zoe could ever be threatened by a loser like me, it made a twisted sort of sense.

"It's like Amanda has some spooky power over her," Jake continued.

My body flinched at the word *power*. What did he mean by that exactly? I held out my hands for the ball, trying to cover my uneasiness. He mimed shooting a lay-up, then dribbled a few times before passing the ball back to me. "So that girl who died. You were friends with her, right?"

"Tabitha?" I caught the ball and held it.

"Tabitha."

"She was my best friend." I turned the ball slowly in my hands. I wasn't saying it to impress him. I was saying it because it was true. And as I said it, I realized that as much as I was loving sitting there with Jake, as much as it was basically the realization of my deepest, strongest dream ever, the one I'd never had while I was sleeping but walked around having every hour I was awake, I'd trade it in a heartbeat to be sitting there with Tabitha, talking about how hopeless it was to imagine Jake even knew I was alive.

"Tell me if it's none of my business, but what happened the night she died?"

"How should I know?" My butt was hurting from the steps. I threw the ball back at him with force. The ticking of the clock in my brain got a little harder to ignore.

"I thought you were there." Jake returned the pass easily.

Tick, tick.

I remembered Ms. Labos saying the boys had met the girls at the pool. "I thought *you* were there." I shot the ball back.

Tick, tick.

Jake shook his head, dribbling some more, jogging in circles around the ball. A guy walking a dog approached and the dog barked at the ball excitedly. Jake stepped into the gutter to let them go by. "We didn't get there until after. Amanda told us to meet them at the pool, they had some surprise for us, but by the time we got there, the cops had the pool closed off, so we just left."

Brrrrring! went the alarm in my brain.

"What was the surprise?"

"I don't know." He stepped back onto the sidewalk and looked down at the ball in his hands, thinking. "None of them will say. Zoe says they've all taken a vow of silence about that night or something. I think I'm not supposed to be talking about it either.

They talked to the cops, but they won't tell anyone what they said."

"Except somehow the whole school knows that Amanda told the cops Tabitha left the party to meet me, and then was acting weird when she came back, and that's when she dived into the pool and hit her head."

"But that's not what happened?" Jake frowned at the ball, like he could see the swimming pool in its pebbly orange skin.

I was opening my mouth to say that was what I was there to talk to Zoe about, when suddenly the ball flew out of Jake's hands and smacked me in the face.

"Ow!" I yelped, covering my nose with my hands. My eyes filled with tears and my upper lip began tingling.

"Dude, are you okay?" Jake rushed over. "I am so sorry! I have no idea how that happened. Can I look?" Before I could stop him, Jake was pulling my hands away from my nose. As much as it hurt, I wasn't too injured to feel a little fizz of excitement at being touched by him.

"What's going on?" Zoe said. Neither of us had heard her walk up, and we both jumped.

"I just accidentally beaned your friend," Jake said, continuing to examine my nose. "The ball slipped out of my hands." He pulled a tissue out of his pocket and wiped my lip. When he took it away, the tissue was streaked with blood.

"Here." Zoe took a handkerchief out of her bag, twisted one end, and told me to shove it in my nostril. I obeyed, my hands shaking, and not just from the shock of being hit in the face or the embarrassment of having Jake see me with a handkerchief stuffed up my nose.

Had the ball really slipped out of Jake's hands?

Or had Zoe heard us talking and made the ball hit me to shut me up?

"I am so sorry, Tess," Jake said, but he'd already stopped looking at me and was now pulling Zoe to him for a big, sloppy kiss. If he'd been annoyed at her before, he'd forgiven her in a hurry.

Zoe had her eyes open as he kissed her, but she refused to meet my eyes.

"Where you been?" Jake said, once they stopped kissing.

"The subway's a mess, I told you." Zoe flipped her hair behind her shoulder. She was trying to act cool, but her voice trembled, and her eyes were wild. "I was stuck on the 6 for like forty minutes."

"Are you okay?" Jake asked, cupping her face with his hand. "You look all shook up."

"I'm fine." Zoe brushed away his hand. "I think someone jumped on the tracks."

"For real?" Jake walked to the gutter to retrieve the basketball from where it had rolled under a car. "Why do people do that? I mean, if you're going to kill yourself, why inconvenience everyone else who doesn't want to die?" He walked back to the stoop and balanced the ball on the step, eyeing it warily like it might leap up and attack someone else. "You, stay," he said to it.

"Totally." Zoe wrapped her arms around his neck and picked up her feet to swing from him like he was her own personal jungle gym. She gave him another kiss, closing her eyes this time, and I had to look away. It hurt to see them together, even if, according to her, they didn't even like each other anymore.

They sure seemed to like each other right then. Or at least he sure seemed to like her. He set her down on the ground carefully, like she might break, even though I was the one with the bloody nose.

Zoe turned to me. "Did we have plans to hang out?"

Jake had hooked his fingers through the loops of her waistband and was pulling her hips toward him, then pushing her away, and I realized they were waiting for me to leave so they could go have sex.

"No. I just needed to talk to you about something."

Zoe gave me an expectant look. Jake picked up his basketball again.

"It's just . . ." My nose was throbbing, like it was starting to swell. I was sure the ball hadn't slipped out of Jake's hands.

Or had it?

"I just wanted to know what time practice is Monday," I said finally.

"It's at four thirty," Zoe said with a big, fake smile.

"Great! Thanks!" I said, trying to sound as fake cheery as she did. "It's such a drag not having my phone." I rolled my eyes. "I'll wash this and get it back to you," I added, stuffing the bloody handkerchief in my pocket.

"Sorry again about that," Jake said, already pulling Zoe up the steps toward her door. "I have no idea what happened. It literally jumped out of my hands."

I was about to correct his use of *literally* when I realized he was actually right.

"Yeah, it was like it had a mind of its own," I said, locking eyes with Zoe.

"You know, you can just keep the handkerchief," she said. Was she blushing? "Hope you find your phone."

"Thanks," I said. "And thanks for letting me know about practice."

I had no intention of going to practice, and I had no intention of talking to Zoe again, if I could help it. If I was going to find out how Tabitha had died, I was going to have to do it by myself.

CHAPTER THIRTY-EIGHT

The next morning I got up early and went for a long run along the Hudson all the way up to the lighthouse below the George Washington Bridge. I might not have been on the team anymore, but I needed to clear my head, and even though I should have stayed in bed and tried to catch up on sleep, I couldn't stand hanging around the apartment, wondering if my dad was speaking to me again.

The Hudson was a steely gray, but the sun kept peeking through the clouds, turning the river silver and making the bridge shine in the distance. I pushed myself to run fast, spotting joggers ahead and then picking up my pace until I passed them. It had been way too long since I'd had a real workout, and everything hurt, but the pain gave me something to focus on.

Every time I thought about Zoe, or Amanda, or Tabitha dead in the pool, or my mom, or my own encroaching mental instability, I forced myself to go faster, until the agony in my muscles drowned out the questions in my brain.

After about three miles my legs stopped complaining, and I could feel my lungs stretching out, expanding to process my breath more efficiently. It was chilly by the water, but I took off my fleece, letting the salty breeze draw pinprick goosebumps on my arms and smack against my face like a slap.

At the lighthouse I turned and headed back toward home, without even stopping for water. By the top of Riverside Park, my legs were feeling heavy, but I didn't want to slow down. I took my iPod out of the pocket of my fleece and put it on shuffle.

"Little Bitch" by The Specials came on. I immediately hit the forward button. The next song was David Bowie, "Young Americans."

"Shit!" I said and pulled the earbuds out of my ears. The official *Sixteen Candles* soundtrack had only five tracks on it, but for my fourteenth birthday, Tabitha had found the rest of the songs on YouTube and made me a mix.

Hearing the opening bars of the two songs made me realize how long it had been since I'd watched the movie, since I'd listened to my iPod, since I'd done any of the things I used to do all the time, without thinking, when Tabitha was alive.

In the movie, Caroline tells Jake, "I owe all my great weekends to you." Maybe Tabitha and I hadn't done anything all that special when we were together, but any semblance of a normal social life I'd had, I owed to her.

I'd never gotten to thank her.

Tears filled in my eyes, but it could've been the wind. I wiped my face with my palms. Suddenly I was furious. I put my earbuds back in and forwarded the songs until I came to "Little Bitch" again.

I sang along under my breath, willing my legs to go faster, to make it hurt: "And you think it's about time you died, and I agree, so you decide on suicide . . . and if you think you're gonna bleed all over me, you're even wronger than you'd normally be . . . I know you know you're just a little bitch!"

I was singing to Zoe.

To Amanda.

To Tabitha.

To myself.

CHAPTER THIRTY-NINE

I let myself into the apartment still breathing hard, trying to hang onto the feeling of motion and release, trying to postpone the moment of crashing back to reality.

Ms. Labos was sitting on the sofa. A man in a coat and tie sat next to her. My dad was in the chair across from them. I could tell from the silence they had been waiting for me.

Crash.

I very much wanted to turn around and run back to the lighthouse, climb inside, and refuse to come out.

If my legs hadn't been cooked, I might have.

Instead, I went into the kitchen and got myself a glass of water and washed my face at the sink, then dried it with a paper towel. I went back into the living room.

"Tess, sit down." Ms. Labos's voice was calm and low, an utterly successful impersonation of an adult. She was wearing jeans and a sweatshirt, which somehow made her look much older than her workday suits and pantyhose did.

I sat.

My dad wouldn't look at me.

"We have some questions for you, and we need you to be honest with us this time," Ms. Labos said.

"I was honest with you before," I said, more to my dad than Ms. Labos.

"We know you weren't."

A cup of coffee sat on the table in front of Ms. Labos, its rim marred by a lipstick kiss. It was nearly full. My dad's coffee is an acquired taste.

"And that's okay." The man in the necktie leaned forward. He reached for his own coffee cup, then thought better and pulled back his hand. "You were probably in shock and confused about what had happened. But now that a little more time has passed, we need you to tell us the entire truth. There's nothing to be afraid of."

"Tess, this is Detective O'Ryan," Ms. Labos said.

Up to that point I had assumed he was someone else from school. The word *detective* scared me. I looked at my dad again. He caught my eye this time and gave me a wavering smile.

"You're not in trouble, sweetie. You just need to tell them what really happened the night Tabitha died."

"I told you. We had a fight on the phone. She said she was going to a party for Amanda. I went to sleep." I wondered if I should tell them about my vision, let them know how crazy I was.

Innocent by reason of insanity.

"But then you woke up," Ms. Labos prompted, as if reading my thoughts.

"Yes," I said slowly. "Then I woke up."

"And you sent Tabitha a text," Detective O'Ryan said.

I nodded, looking at my dad.

"And when she wrote back, you said you needed to talk to her, and you'd meet her outside the party."

"That's not true!" I said.

"Two of the girls who were there that night say that's what happened," Ms. Labos said.

"But . . . but they're lying." I looked at my dad, waiting for him to interrupt and say I didn't have to answer any more questions and he wanted them out of the house immediately. But he was just watching me, like he was as interested in my answers as they were. Jujube was curled in a tight ball on one of the chairs in the kitchen. He was pretending to be asleep, but I could tell he was listening to every word.

"Why would they lie?" Ms. Labos asked gently.

It was the question I had been asking myself. The question for which I had no good answer. "I don't know," I admitted. "Maybe Amanda's lying because she doesn't want you to know they were drinking at the pool," I said slowly. "And Zoe's lying because she's afraid of Amanda."

Ms. Labos and the detective looked at each other. Even I knew how preposterous it sounded. Amanda hated me, no doubt, but enough to implicate me in Tabitha's death? The other option—that I was completely insane—seemed far more likely. But was I so insane that I had met Tabitha at the pool and then completely forgotten about it?

Detective O'Ryan sighed and ran a hand over his face. "We know the girls were drinking, and we'll deal with that appropriately," he said. "But we also know Tabitha left the school briefly at one point and returned a few minutes later."

"You do?" My dad leaned forward, looking worried.

"There's a security camera above the main entrance," Ms. Labos said. "Unfortunately, it got knocked off balance, so it only records the area directly in front of the doors. The footage shows Tabitha leaving at, what, two thirty?" She looked at the detective. He pulled a folded-up piece of paper from his breast pocket, unfolded it, and scanned it.

"Two thirty-seven A.M.," he said. "And returning at two fifty-five A.M."

"But you don't see her actually meeting anyone?" My dad's eyes were narrowed, and I could tell he was going into lawyer mode. I hoped Ms. Labos and Detective O'Ryan didn't know my dad mostly did tax law.

"No," said the detective. "We just have two witnesses saying that she met someone."

"But not eyewitnesses," my dad said. "So technically that's just hearsay. And anyway, Tess says they're lying."

I shot him a grateful glance. He may have been mad at me for the way I'd treated my mom at the hospital, but he still believed me. He was still on my side.

"So, to be clear, you're saying you didn't meet Tabitha, and you also didn't send her a text asking you to meet?" the detective asked.

I looked at my dad. I pulled on my streak, then, realizing they were all watching me, dropped my hand. I nodded.

"But you did text her?"

I nodded again. This, at least, I remembered.

"What did the text say?"

"It said, *you're never going to believe this, but I had this very bizarre dream and you were in it.*" I kept my eyes on the floor, waiting for them to ask me what my dream had been.

Ms. Labos laughed softly. "*Sixteen Candles*, right?"

I looked up, surprised, and she smiled at me, a quick, tentative smile. "It was our favorite movie," I said.

"Look, if Tess says she didn't meet Tabitha, she didn't meet her," my dad said. "I don't see how the private communication between two teenagers is any of your business, so if you're done with your questions . . ."

Detective O'Ryan held up a hand, interrupting him. "It's our business because the coroner found drugs in Tabitha's bloodstream, and we think whoever met her gave them to her."

"What?" my dad and I said at the same time.

"That's why we're here, Tess," Ms. Labos said. She'd stopped smiling and looked like an adult again. "We got back the toxicology report. This isn't about whether you and Tabitha were in a fight, or who said what to who." She shot me a look. "Whom?"

I nodded.

"This is about who is responsible for her death," the detective finished for her.

"Wait," my dad said. "Are you saying you think Tabitha was murdered?"

Detective O'Ryan held out his hands in a "whoa" gesture. "All we're saying is, we know Tabitha left the pool. We have several reports that she was acting strange when she returned. Our working theory is, she got a text from someone asking her to come outside, and that person then gave her drugs. So the question is, if Tess didn't meet her, who did?"

Before any of us could answer, Jujube came running into the room and jumped into Ms. Labos's lap. He turned around and around, rubbing his tail in her face, purring wildly. Ms. Labos waved her hands in the air, then sneezed.

"Jujube! Get down!" My dad grabbed Juju and tossed him on the floor, and Juju immediately leaped back onto Ms. Labos, purring frantically. Ms. Labos sneezed again. Juju kept winding himself under her arms and out of her hands like a fur-covered eel, determined to stay on her lap as she struggled to shove him down.

"I'm so sorry!" My dad pulled at Juju's hind legs while he dug his front claws into the arm of the sofa. "He's normally very sedate." He let go of one of Juju's legs to pry his claws out of the sofa, and Juju immediately leaped back onto Ms. Labos's lap. "Are you a cat person?" my dad asked weakly.

"No, I . . . I . . . achoo!" Ms. Labos pushed Jujube's tail out from under her nose. "I love cats. I'm just—achoo!—very—achoo!—allergic." Next to her, Detective O'Ryan recoiled, like her allergies might be contagious. He was definitely not a cat person.

"Enough, beast." My dad wrapped both arms around the cat and pulled with all his might. All at once Juju released his claws from the sofa, and my dad staggered backward. Once he regained his balance, he threw Juju over his shoulder and headed for the bedroom. Suddenly docile, Juju rode quietly against my dad, looking at me from over my dad's shoulder. Right before my dad threw him in the bedroom and shut the door, Juju winked.

Ms. Labos was sneezing so violently the coffee cups were rattling on the table.

"Let me get you some tissue," my dad said.

He started rummaging in the kitchen while Ms. Labos continued to sneeze and sniffle and drip, and Detective O'Ryan just sat there, looking disgusted. He picked a clump of cat fur off the knee of his pants and flicked it to the floor.

"I guess we're out," my dad said from the kitchen. "There's toilet paper in the bathroom, if you want . . ."

Still sneezing, Ms. Labos got up and ran toward the bathroom, holding her hands over her nose. My dad came back in the room, and we all sat there, listening to the honking sounds of her blowing her nose, followed by running water. After a few moments the sneezes stopped.

"Anyway, Tess, do you have any idea who might have met Tabitha?" Detective O'Ryan peered at me, then wiped his nose. "Achoo!"

"Don't tell me you're allergic, too," my dad said.

"I'm not. But that is one furry cat." He turned to me. "Tess?"

I took a deep breath.

"Dess? Can you come in here a binute?" Ms. Labos called from the bathroom. I gave my dad a puzzled look, and he shrugged at me.

"Okay."

Ms. Labos opened the bathroom door and let me in, then shut it behind her. Her eyes were puffy slits, and her nose was red and drippy. She was breathing through her mouth. "I bas booking to see if you had any Claritin."

"Hang on." I knelt in front of the cabinet under the sink. After rifling around a few moments, I found a bottle of nasal spray and handed it up to her. She squirted spray into each nostril, tilted her head back, and swallowed.

"Tanks," she said, giving me back the spray. She swallowed again, rubbed her nose, and exhaled. "While I was looking, I found these." Her voice was back to normal, but her eyes were still swollen nearly shut. She sounded worried.

Before I could say anything, she opened the medicine cabinet above the sink. I didn't have to look to know what she'd seen. Rows and rows of little tan bottles of pills.

"They're my mom's." I stayed crouched in front of the cabinet, my back to her.

"But you had access to them," she said. "I'm not a pharmacist, but I bet most of these are strong enough to make someone fall in a pool, especially if she'd been drinking."

The blood rushed from my head. I understood what she was saying. Every crime needs a means, motive, and opportunity. My fight with Tabitha was the motive. If she'd left the pool to meet me, like Amanda and Zoe said, that would have been my opportunity. And Ms. Labos had just found the means.

"This isn't looking good for you," Ms. Labos said.

"I know," I said, sinking all the way to the floor. I put my face in my hands.

She shut the medicine cabinet. "If Detective O'Ryan sees this he might even arrest you," she whispered, then sniffled.

I was only sixteen. Maybe they wouldn't try me as an adult, and I'd wind up in juvenile hall. Maybe I'd meet some other kids there. Kids who were crazy. Kids who were freaks. Kids like me.

"I want to help you. But you have to tell me what happened."
Ms. Labos squatted in front of me and put a hand on my shoulder.

"I swear, I've told you everything," I said. Everything I remembered, at least.

"Can you think of anyone who might know anything more?"

I leaned my head back against the tiled wall and closed my eyes. I gave my streak a tentative little pull. It was tempting to confess I had met Tabitha outside the pool, had given her the drugs that killed her.

Everyone thought that was what had happened.

Was it?

"Yes." I opened my eyes. "I think, maybe, I can."

CHAPTER FORTY

By the time we got off the subway at West 4th Street, Ms. Labos's eyes had returned to their normal size, and she was only sniffling occasionally. Her allergy attack had convinced Detective O'Ryan to save the rest of his questions for another day, and, after giving my dad his card and Juju a very dirty look, he'd left, saying he'd be in touch soon. In the meantime, I had to get some answers.

The sun had burned through the clouds, and it had turned into a pretty late-fall day, with that crispness to the air that signals winter is right around the corner, but you'll get a few more days of warmth before the chill sets in for good.

We crossed the street to the park, where a group of guys were playing basketball with their shirts off. A bunch of spectators hung around outside the fence, watching the game. Ms. Labos joined the crowd and threaded her fingers through the chain links, so I did the same.

"Oh my God," she said.

"What?"

"Eli Boylan."

I peered through the fence. Some of the guys playing were old, with the beginnings of pot bellies and hair in weird places on their bodies, but others were young, like my age, tall and skinny and practically hairless.

It didn't take long to spot Jake in the crowd, all sweaty and shimmery and glowing with his special gorgeousness. He loped up and down the court, dribbling easily, then did a bounce pass to the guy running next to him, who was a shorter, bulkier, darker-haired version of Jake.

Not as gorgeous, but just as graceful. A little rougher looking. But definitely cute. He must have been Jake's older brother, Eli.

"Do you know him?"

"We were in school together." Ms. Labos swallowed hard.

Poor Ms. Labos. Of course she'd loved Eli, the way I loved Jake. To every dork her prince. It was just so pathetic that she was still mooning over him all these years later. I doubted he'd even known her name in high school.

After a few more minutes, the game broke up and Jake jogged toward us, dribbling the ball. When he got within a few feet, he made an exaggerated show of picking up the ball and carrying it carefully with both hands, holding it out in front of him like it was a bomb.

"Hi, Ms. Labos. Hey, Tess. Maybe I should leave this here?" He put the ball down on the ground with the same exaggerated care. I smiled in spite of myself, feeling stupidly happy that he had remembered hitting me in the face, as embarrassing as it had been.

"Funny how I keep running into you," he said, and my smile turned into a blush.

"Actually, your mom told us you were down here," Ms. Labos said. "Got a sec?"

Just then Eli walked up. I could feel Ms. Labos stiffen beside me.

"Who's your friend?" Eli asked his brother, looking at me. His eyes were just as mesmerizing as Jake's. I reached up and tugged on my streak for strength. Then he noticed Ms. Labos.

"Oh, hey, Heather. What's up?"

Ms. Labos drew her shoulders back and sucked in her breath. If she'd had a streak, she would have been tugging on it, too. Instead, she said, in her most robotic school counselor voice, "Hello, Eli. We have some questions for Jake. It's official school business."

Official school business? With that, she erased the years between them and high school and was back to being a floundering geek, a loser through and through. She must've known how ridiculous she sounded, because she turned an eggplanty shade of purple.

Eli burst out laughing. "Official school business? What are you, the crossing guard?"

I could have died for Ms. Labos right then. If anyone knew how she felt, I did.

"My friend died," I said. "And now the cops think she might have been murdered. And Jake was involved. So it's pretty serious."

Eli looked at Jake. "Dude?" he said, furrowing his brow. "Dude."

● ● ●

Jake and Eli were starving, so we went across the street to Papaya Dog. At first I was too self-conscious to eat in front of Jake, but after he and his brother had inhaled two dogs apiece, I couldn't ignore my hunger pangs any longer. I hadn't eaten anything since my run, and I was woozy from low blood sugar. I got a hot dog and a mango shake and felt a little better after a few bites.

Ms. Labos explained to Jake that we needed to know everything he knew about the night Tabitha died. She said he didn't need to worry about us getting him in trouble—that no matter what he said, about drinking or drugs or breaking into the pool, it would be okay, but she couldn't promise the same if he told his story to Detective O'Ryan. It was a classic *Law and Order* speech, but he appeared to buy it.

The whole time she was talking, Eli just kept smirking at her, but he didn't say anything. When she was done, he nudged Jake with his elbow, like, *go on, spill it.*

Jake swallowed the last bites of his third hot dog and wiped his mouth with his napkin. Next to his brother and Ms. Labos, he looked young—unformed. But he also had that sparkly glow that neither Ms. Labos nor Eli had anymore. Eli had probably glowed when he was at Whitman, too, but in the years since graduation it had slowly worn off.

Ms. Labos, I was certain, had never glowed.

In the fluorescent light of the Papaya Dog I could see that Eli's hair was beginning to thin on top, and soft little pouches of loose skin were gathering at his jowls. He'd never be as beautiful as his brother again.

"I don't know any more than I told Tess." Jake slurped up the last of his soda. "Amanda texted that they were all at the pool, and we should meet them there because they had a surprise for us."

"Do you hang out at the pool often?" Ms. Labos asked.

Jake glanced at Eli. Eli ducked his head, like, *go ahead.*

"Pretty often."

Eli gave a little snort. "As in, every weekend, right?"

Jake nodded.

"And there's usually drinking?" Ms. Labos asked.

Jake nodded again.

"Anything else?"

Jake scratched his head. "You mean, like, swimming?"

"Like any drugs."

"Not usually."

"Bullshit," Eli coughed into his fist.

"Sometimes kids do molly, but no one was on it that night that I know of."

"Okay, so this surprise. Do you have any idea what it was?" Ms. Labos asked.

"No. No idea."

"And Zoe hasn't told you anything since then?"

"No." He shook his head violently. "She barely tells me anything anymore. Ever since that night, it's like she's afraid to be alone with me. She's just being weird in general."

"Dude," Eli said, "you could go out with any girl you want. You don't need to put up with that from any chick."

I fought to keep from jumping up and applauding.

Jake shook his head. "You don't understand. I love her. We're soul mates. She's just going through a hard time." My heart died a little bit at his words. No guy would ever, ever call me his soul mate.

"So Zoe considered Tabitha a close friend?" Ms. Labos sipped her drink. She hadn't looked directly at Eli once the whole time we'd been talking.

Jake wadded up his napkin, threw it in the air, then batted it to the table. "I wouldn't exactly say that."

"Tabitha was more Amanda's friend?"

Jake barked a laugh. "I definitely wouldn't say that."

"Then why was she at the pool that night?"

"I know! That's what I kept asking Zoe. I mean, I think Tabitha *thought* she was friends with them, but they didn't actually like her. They were just letting her think they'd accepted her, but they talked about her behind her back all the time. You know how girls are about that stuff." He looked at me.

I was about to say no, I didn't know how girls are about that stuff, when I realized I was just as guilty of being two-faced as Zoe and Amanda were. I put down my hot dog. My stomach didn't feel so good.

It should have made me happy to hear that Tabitha hadn't actually made herself into a Caroline—it should have felt like vindication. But it felt awful. All I could hope was that she had died without knowing how Zoe and Amanda really felt about her. That she had died thinking she'd done it, the change was real, and that she was actually as happy as she'd said she was the last time we talked on the phone.

Eli raised his eyebrows at the stub of hot dog on my plate. I passed it over to him.

"Keep going," Ms. Labos said. She was weirdly good at this. Maybe being a guidance counselor taught her how to get kids to talk.

"Just that, they thought she was annoying, the way she tagged along after them. And then when she went out for track? They really didn't like that."

"But they still let her come to Amanda's party."

Jake twisted his straw wrapper around his finger thoughtfully. "You know, the only other thing I remember is right before the party, Tabitha kept texting Zoe and Amanda. Like, constantly. We were at Zoe's house, and her phone would buzz, and then ten seconds later Amanda's phone would buzz, and she'd have sent practically the same text to each of them, with just a few words changed. Not saying anything important. Like, I think she wrote to Amanda that the party was going to be *super fun*"—he wiggled his fingers in air quotes—"and then she wrote to Zoe that the party was going to be *major fun*." He wiggled his fingers again. "So they started making fun of her for that. Zoe would be like, *does this shirt look super good?* And Amanda would be like, *no, it looks major good.* And then Amanda was like, *is it just me, or is Tabitha major lame?* And Zoe said *no, Tabitha is super lame,* and they decided she was super major lame."

They would've been lying on Zoe's bed, their hair hanging off the edge, bored, looking for an excuse to laugh and act stupid. Except for the part about Jake being there to witness it, it was a scene that Tabitha and I had played out in her bedroom a hundred times over the last years. It wasn't fair that she was dead, and they were still alive to be bored and stupid together.

"Anyway, Zoe was like, *how much longer do we have to put up with this*, and Amanda was like, *just this weekend*, or something," Jake continued. "I didn't think anything about it at the time, but I don't know, do you think it had anything to do with what happened?"

Eli was staring at Jake. He looked at Ms. Labos. "Ya think?" he said.

I couldn't tell if Eli was being sarcastic or not. Ms. Labos just looked sad, like hearing Jake talk about the way Amanda and Zoe had treated Tabitha had reminded her of something, too. Maybe of her dorky high-school self. Maybe like me, she felt bad that Tabitha hadn't succeeded at transforming herself into a popular girl.

Or maybe it was just killing her to be so close to Eli, the way it would have been killing me to be so close to Jake if I hadn't been too curious about what had happened that night at the pool.

"And when you try to ask Zoe about it she won't tell you anything?" Ms. Labos asked.

"Like I said, they all took a vow of silence. She would be super mad if she knew I was even talking to you," Jake said.

"Super mad or major mad?" I said, but no one laughed. I guess it wasn't that funny.

CHAPTER FORTY-ONE

Ms. Labos said she'd call Zoe and Amanda in the morning and see if she could use the threat of Detective O'Ryan to get them to tell her what the "surprise" had been. And if I thought of anyone else who might have met Tabitha that night, I should call her anytime.

I should have felt relieved that she believed I hadn't been at the pool that night, but I still wasn't sure *I* believed it. It didn't help that Ms. Labos had seen all the pills in the medicine cabinet. For the rest of the evening, my stomach churned with undigested hot dog, and I kept catching myself pulling on my streak without even realizing it. I was sure I wouldn't sleep at all, but I passed out as soon as I lay down on my bed.

• • •

I woke up a few hours later with my mom sitting on my bed, petting my hair. I opened my eyes and she smiled at me. She looked so pretty and so young, like in the pictures from when my parents first met.

My dad had been a corporate lawyer, working at one of the big firms in Midtown. His firm was a sponsor of Shakespeare in the Park, and all the employees got tickets. My dad went on opening night of *A Midsummer Night's Dream*. He thought one of the fairies was the prettiest girl he'd ever seen, and he talked his way backstage after the show. The guy who played Puck was sitting in the dressing room, taking off his makeup, and as my dad waited for the fairy to come in, Puck took off his hat and brushed out his hair, and my dad saw he was actually a woman, and ten times more beautiful than the fairy he had come backstage to find.

He convinced her to go out with him that night. Three months later, they were married.

Lying in bed looking up at my mom, with the streetlights in the window caught in the curls of her hair, and her smile soft and just a little mysterious, and her eyes shiny and clear, I understood completely how my dad could have fallen in love with her the first time he met her.

More than that, I understood how he could still love her, in spite of everything, in spite of having given up his career for her. In spite of worrying about her all the time, in spite of the fact that we all were prisoners to her illness. I saw that she was a prisoner, too, but that underneath it all she was still herself, beautiful and serene.

She smelled good, like her old shampoo, and when she saw my eyes were open, she crinkled her nose at me, just like she used to do when I was little, when we'd give each other bunny kisses.

"Why aren't you in the hospital?"

"I checked myself out," she whispered.

"Can you do that?"

She shrugged coyly, raising one shoulder and dropping her chin.

"So are you better?" Something about it being the middle of the night, and the only light coming from the street, made it okay to talk like this about her sickness.

She reached out and petted my hair. "I was never as sick as they thought. They say it's a sickness because they don't know what else to call it. But it's not illness. It's magic."

"So Grandma was right?"

She nodded. "Of course."

"But all the pills . . ."

"I had to go along with them. What if I told them the truth? It would just prove that I was crazy. I was worried they would take you away from me. Or convince your dad it wasn't safe for me to be around you. So I let them prescribe me pills. I took them sometimes. It never made any difference anyway. The magic is much stronger than anything doctors can come up with."

"Is Grandma right about me, too?"

She nodded.

"Why didn't you tell me?"

She smiled her special smile then, the one that said *it's you and me against the world, and together nothing can stop us.* "I had to wait for you to discover it on your own." She stroked my streak, then took it in her hand and gave it a tug.

She looked out the window and sighed, and for a moment she looked like a curtain of despair had been drawn over her face. She took a breath, gave my streak another tug, and smiled at me. "I love you so much, my magical, magical girl."

"I love you, too."

"It hasn't all been bad, has it? We've had some happy times, too. Like at Grandma's cabin in the summer, on the lake . . . remember how we used to swim out to the dock?"

For a moment I saw the blue water, felt the warm sun, the heat off my mother's tanned arm next to mine as we baked side by side on the dock.

Then a cloud obscured the memory, cold and gray, and I shivered in my bed.

"I have to go now. But don't be sad. It's best for everyone. Best for you, best for your dad. You'll be fine, just wait and see."

"Where are you going?" I struggled to sit up, but her hands were pinning me against the pillow. I always forget how strong she is.

"Just . . . away. But don't worry about me. I won't be alone."

"Away where?"

"To be with Tabitha."

"No!" I fought against her hands. "I don't want you to leave! You just got home! I want you to stay!"

Her smile changed, grew crafty and cold, and she pushed me against the pillows and stood up from the bed.

"I think you want me to leave. I think that's what you really want, just like you wanted Tabitha to die and you wanted Finn to hurt Zoe. That's why you're having this dream, isn't it? You want me gone, too."

"No!" I shouted, but she had already turned and walked out the door, and I was sitting up in bed, shouting into the darkness, alone.

CHAPTER FORTY-TWO

The nurse at the front desk of the hospital was reading *Us Weekly* and eating a burrito. It was the middle of the night, but I guess it was lunchtime for him. After I stood there for a minute, shifting my weight and making little interrupting sounds, he sighed heavily and looked up. The front of his light-blue scrubs was spotted with either blood or salsa.

"I'm on break," he said. "The on-duty nurse will be back in a minute. You can wait over there." He waved his burrito toward the waiting area. A few grains of rice fell onto a picture of Jennifer Lawrence in a bikini.

"This is sort of an emergency?" I said.

The nurse picked up the rice, grain by grain, placing each slowly in his mouth, chewing and swallowing, before looking at me again. "There's no sort-of emergency. Either it's an emergency, or you're wasting my time."

"My mom. Sylvia Block. I think she's in trouble." Then, before he could question my syntax again, I corrected myself. "She's in trouble."

The nurse turned to his computer and slowly began typing. "Susan Black?"

"Sylvia."

"Sylvia Black."

"Block. Sylvia Block."

He typed some more. "Huh."

"Did you find her?"

"Yup."

"Can you check on her?"

"Nope." He went back to his magazine.

"I'm serious. This is an emergency," I said, leaning over the counter. I wanted to rip the magazine out of his hands. "You need to check on her."

"I told you, I can't," the nurse said, without lifting his eyes.

"What about the other nurse?"

"Nope."

"Why not?"

"Your mom's not here. She checked herself out an hour ago."

"Oh."

The nurse held his burrito in front of his mouth, preparing for another bite, and raised his eyebrows, daring me to interrupt again.

"Did she say where she was going?"

The nurse shrugged. "I wasn't on duty then."

"Well, does it say anything about where she went?"

He sighed, put down the burrito, and returned to the computer. "Checked herself out to own care." He looked up. "We can't make them stay, you know, unless they're here under involuntary commitment. She checked herself in, she can check herself out. Doesn't have to tell us where she's going or anything." He looked at the computer again. "Oh, that's weird."

"What?"

"She forgot to take her stuff."

"What do you mean?"

"Her stuff. When they check in they hand over anything they can hurt themselves with, and we give it back to them when they leave."

"Like jail?"

The nurse looked at me like I was the stupidest person he'd ever met. "You can't check yourself out of jail."

He leaned over and pulled open the drawer of a filing cabinet. He came back up with a gallon plastic baggie with a piece of masking tape on it. *Sylvia Block* was written on the tape. "Yep, here it is. Guess she was in a hurry, or she thought she'd be coming back soon."

Or she didn't think she'd need it anymore.

"Can I have it?"

The nurse squinted at me. He glanced at his burrito and his magazine. "You're her daughter?"

I nodded.

"You're eighteen?"

I nodded again. Sometimes having a white streak can work to my advantage.

The nurse shrugged, handed over the bag and a clipboard. "Sign this."

I signed.

My hand was shaking.

Through the translucent plastic of the bag I could see my phone.

CHAPTER FORTY-THREE

I turned the phone on in the elevator. My mom hadn't even bothered to delete the conversation with Tabitha. I saw the last thing I had written:

I had this very bizarre dream and you were in it.

Then:

I need to talk to you.
Can we talk about this tomorrow?
I need to talk to you tonight. Are you still at Amanda's?
No.
Where are you?
At the Whitman pool.
Meet me outside. I'll text when I get there. It will just take a minute.
Fine. Text when you get here.

Then . . .

Here.

CHAPTER FORTY-FOUR

The street in front of the hospital was artificially bright with the lights from the lobby and the flashing lights of an ambulance idling in front of the ER. Doctors and nurses walked in and out, chatting and sipping Starbucks as though it were the middle of the day, but outside the cone of activity in front of the hospital, the street was dark and quiet.

Taxis streamed up First Avenue, their VACANT lights on, and a street sweeper rumbled along the curb, pushing trash and soot onto the sidewalk.

By the time I got to the corner, I was so dizzy I had to reach out and hold the lightbox for support. A homeless woman collecting cans from the wire trashcan asked if I was okay. I nodded, though I wasn't okay at all.

Up the block, a neon shamrock with one leaf burned out blinked above the door of a pub. I went in.

It was as dark and murky inside as the bottom of a dirty aquarium, and I had to grope my way up onto the stool. The bar was sticky to my touch. There was a dish of pretzels at one end. I couldn't imagine anyone drinking enough to think eating them was a good idea. Then again, the hospital was nearby.

The bartender was talking to an old guy in a newsboy cap slumped at the end of the bar, but when she saw me she knocked on the bar, then walked over. She had white hair hanging down her back and tattoos up both arms. She reminded me of a punk version of my grandmother.

"What can I get you?" She reached under the bar for a glass.

"A beer, please." The sound of my voice made her look at me. "Are you twenty-one?"

I had been eighteen just a few minutes ago. "Twenty-two."

She considered me for another moment. "You're sure about that?"

I tugged on my streak. "I'm old enough to have this, aren't I?"

She shrugged, as though overpowered by my logic, and asked what kind of beer I wanted. I glanced at the taps over her shoulder and ordered a Stella, the first name I saw. She poured me the beer, put it on a small napkin in front of me, and pushed the pretzels closer.

"I don't believe you," she said, "but you look like you could use this. So drink it and get out of here, okay? Almost last call anyway."

I put the bag of my mom's stuff on the bar in front of me. I saw her hairbrush, with a few strands wound around the bristles. There was a small disk of dental floss—how was that lethal? I guess, if you wanted to die badly enough, you could use anything. There was a small bottle of mouthwash and a pair of socks I recognized because I'd been there when my grandmother had knitted them for her.

My mom had been wearing slippers when I visited her. Maybe she surrendered the socks because she didn't need them. Or maybe looking at them made her too sad.

I took out my phone to read the texts again, then changed my mind and put it face-down on the bar. I took a big gulp of beer instead. I missed my mom so much it felt like a physical ache. My bones hurt with wanting to see her. It was confusing. I should have never wanted to see her again, now that I knew what she'd done.

I should have been furious at her and missing Tabitha instead, but all I wanted was to be a little girl again, lying in my bed, listening to my mom do her vocalization exercises as she brushed her hair in the bathroom. *Amidst the mists and fiercest frosts, with barest wrists and stoutest boasts, he thrust his fist against the post, and still insists he sees the ghosts.* I wished desperately I had someone to talk to.

Something soft slithered around my ankles. I looked down and saw Jujube curling his tail around my legs. I squeezed my eyes shut, expecting the apparition to resolve itself in the gloom of the bar. When I opened them Juju was still there. The fact that I now believed my cat not only could talk to me but traveled around the city on his own did not bode well for my already deteriorating hold on reality, but I decided to just go with it.

I patted the empty stool next to me and Juju leaped up. I looked up and down the bar. If there was actually a cat on the stool next to me, no one seemed to notice.

"How did you get here?" I whispered, handing him a pretzel.

You've never seen a cat take the subway? He sniffed the pretzel and made a face, then swatted it to the floor with his paw.

"I saw a pigeon riding the A train once."

He flicked his tail dismissively. *Rats with wings. Anyway, you need me. I came.*

"Thanks. Want a drink?"

What are you drinking?

I held the glass down next to him and he took a dainty lick, then made a face again.

What's that, Stella?

I nodded and took another sip. "I don't know what to do."

Tell me what happened.

I told him about my dream, about knowing it meant my mom was going to hurt herself. About going to the hospital to try to save her, but then getting my phone and reading the texts and realizing that she had been the one who met Tabitha outside the pool. I told him that in my dream she had said that I had wanted Tabitha to die and for Zoe to be attacked and for her to die, too.

And that maybe she was right, and maybe I should just let it happen.

She was responsible for my best friend's death. She was crazy. She caused so much pain to my dad, to me, to herself. Maybe it was just best to let my dream come true.

Juju listened, keeping his tail wrapped tight around himself.

Why?

"Why what?"

Why would she meet Tabitha and give her drugs?

"I don't know. All I can think is that she did it for me."

For you?

"That night that Tabitha died. After I had the dream, I went out to the living room. My mom was there on the sofa. I told her everything. I told her what a loser I am. How Tabitha hated me. How *everyone* hates me. How hard it is to go to school every day and then come home and pretend to have friends and be normal, when I actually am an outcast freak."

You're not a freak.

"Yes, I am!" I said, louder than I'd meant to. The bartender glanced at me, then looked at the clock above the television in the corner of the bar. It was quarter to four.

"I am. I know I am," I said more quietly. "Maybe my mom felt bad, like it was her fault, and thought she'd be helping me by getting Tabitha out of the way. Maybe she didn't want her to die. I don't know. Maybe she just did it because she's crazy."

She's also your mom.

"And Tabitha was my best friend."

Not when she died.

"So?"

So, if she'd still been your best friend, you would have tried harder to warn her about your dream. You would have called her and kept calling until she picked up. You would have called Katie and told her to call Amanda's mom and figure out where they were. You would have sent a text telling her she was in danger, not some cryptic movie quote.

"You think I let Tabitha die?"

Isn't that what you think?

I slumped on my stool and gave a tiny nod.

You think you let Tabitha die because she didn't want to be friends anymore. And now, if anything happens to your mom, you're going to think it's your fault, too.

"That's all, folks," the bartender called out, flipping on the overhead lights. I turned to Juju, to ask him what he thought I should do, but he had disappeared, and all that was left was the vinyl barstool, cracked and taped over with duct tape, pieces of stuffing sticking out.

CHAPTER FORTY-FIVE

"Okay, hon, I just need a license and a major credit card," the woman behind the 24-hour rental car agency desk said, yawning as she reached out a hand with diamond-bedazzled nails. I'd already filled out the contract, requested a compact, and declined additional insurance. I'd been surprised at how easy it all was.

Too easy.

I took my license and debit card out of my wallet and handed them to the lady. She looked at the license and shook her head.

"Sorry, hon, this is just a learner's permit. You need a real license to rent a car." She looked at my debit card. "And a real credit card." She turned her attention to my face. "And I'm guessing you're not eighteen?"

I shook my head. My birthdate was printed on the driver's permit. My white streak wasn't going to work this time.

"You have to be eighteen to rent a car in New York. I'm sorry, sweetie. Where do you need to go?"

When I told her, she widened her eyes. "Maybe try Port Authority?"

• • •

I sat on a bench outside the car rental place, wondering what to do next, before I remembered I had my phone back. I looked up the bus schedule. The next bus didn't leave until late afternoon.

Too much could happen between now and then.

I had to get to my mom before it was too late.

Every problem has a solution.
I took a breath and sent Zoe a text.

What's up?

She texted back instantly. She probably slept with her phone on her pillow.

I need you to help me.
Why?
Just meet me at the Dunkin' Donuts on 3rd and 20th.
Now?
Now.
Kinda busy.

At six in the morning on a Sunday? I doubted it.

It's important.

My screen was quiet for one minute, two. Then, *can't.* Then, *sorry.* Finally, *:(.*
I tilted my head back and looked at the clouds, which were just turning golden with the rising sun. It was going to be a cold day, but I felt numb.
If you don't come I'll tell Ms. Labos what happened at the pool, I wrote.
There was a pause, then little bubbles as Zoe wrote, then stopped, then wrote again.
And she'll tell the cops, I added, before she could finish her reply. The bubbles stopped.
I know about the surprise, I wrote.
All I really knew was that Zoe had thought she was telling the truth when she said Tabitha left the pool to meet me. And if Zoe hadn't lied about that, maybe I could trust her more than I thought. But first I had to get her to agree to help me.
I waited to see if she'd take the bluff.

The screen was quiet. A bus trundled up to the stop and the driver looked at me, but I waved him on. Across the street, a woman pulled up the grate on a nail salon. A garbage truck rumbled and wheezed its way through the intersection, burly men hanging off the back.

My phone buzzed.

Twenty minutes.

• • •

I went into Dunkin' Donuts and bought coffee, bagels, donuts, and bottles of water for the trip. When Zoe arrived I told her she needed to get us an Uber. She opened her mouth to protest. I saw her eyeing my bulging bag of provisions.

"Just do it."

She began typing into her phone. "Where are we going?"

"Don't worry about it."

She looked up and flipped her hair, exasperated. "I need a destination," she said. "It won't let me make the reservation without saying where we're going. So enough with the drama, okay?"

"Fine." I shrugged. "We're going to Maine."

CHAPTER FORTY-SIX

After spending twenty minutes trying to sweet-talk the driver into turning off the GPS once we crossed the bridge and then another ten minutes making me swear, double promise, and triple vow to pay her back for the ride, Zoe balled up her sweater, shoved it into the corner of the seat, crossed her arms over her seat belt, and fell asleep.

I tried to do the same, but it had been so long since I'd had a decent night's rest, I'd moved beyond mere exhaustion to an adrenalized state of delirium and soon gave up on a nap and stared out the window instead.

Zoe had asked repeatedly why exactly I needed her to come with me, but the truth was I wasn't sure myself. Maybe I thought she owed it to me. Maybe I was scared to go by myself. Maybe it felt safer to have her with me than in the city with Ms. Labos and the cops asking questions. Maybe I just needed someone who could get us a car.

All I knew was that I had to find my mom before she did something bad. And maybe, somehow, it would help to have Zoe with me when I did.

$$\bullet \; \bullet \; \bullet$$

There was a dusting of snow on the ground around my grand-mother's cabin, and the trees looked black and emaciated. A car I didn't recognize was parked in the driveway. When I opened the door, the chill rushed in, sucking all the warmth out of the car in a single gulp. I began shivering immediately.

I always forget how cold it gets in Maine, that merciless cold that goes straight to your bones. It wasn't even December, but the air was shockingly frigid, brittle, and sharp. It smelled like pine needles and frozen mud. Next to me Zoe snapped awake, sucking her breath in.

"Jesus," she said. "You could have told me to bring a warmer coat."

"Sorry." My own coat felt as insubstantial as a lace shawl.

Zoe got out of the car. The driver turned the car around in the driveway and drove away. We both looked up at the cabin. The front door opened and my grandmother came out, wrapping a sweater around herself.

"What are you girls doing standing around in the wind? You'll freeze. Come in," she said. We followed her inside. My toes were already tingling in my boots.

"Sit," my grandmother said, then turned to the stove and began filling the kettle.

I didn't know how to say what I had to say, so I just blurted it out. "My mom. I think she's in trouble."

"Sit." My grandmother pointed to the table again.

"I think she's going to try to kill herself."

Zoe stared at me, her eyes huge. "You could have told me this six hours ago," she said.

"You were sleeping," I snapped back.

"You couldn't have just called?"

"No phone." I gestured around the kitchen, where the most technologically advanced appliance was the analog clock above the stove.

My grandmother came over, put her hands on my shoulders, and guided me to a chair, then pushed me down. Zoe sat, too, still staring at me.

"Your mother's upstairs," my grandmother said quietly. "She's taking a nap."

I took a deep breath, then exhaled. It felt like the first full breath I'd taken in many hours. "How did you get her to sleep?"

"I gave her something."

"Like, drugs?" Zoe asked.

My grandmother smiled. "She'd driven all night. It didn't take much."

The kettle whistled and my grandmother got up and took it from the stove. She took a box of chamomile tea out of the cupboard, put two bags in the teapot, and poured in the boiling water. The dry, floral smell of the tea filled the air. I'd expected her to make us coffee, but maybe she only did that for family.

"So my mom's okay?"

She waited until she'd poured the tea to answer. "She's very upset. She was saying wild things. About your friend who died. About how it was all her fault."

"That's because it was."

Zoe fumbled her teacup, and it rattled against the table, sloshing hot tea.

"Sorry!" She jumped up for a towel. When she came back to the table, her hand shook as she wiped up the tea. "What do you mean, it was her fault?"

"She used my phone to text Tabitha and get her to leave the party and meet her."

"Tabitha told us she was going outside to meet you."

"My mom made her think it was me so she'd come."

"Your mother told you this?" my grandmother asked. Zoe was staring into her mug. I couldn't read the expression on her face.

"No," I admitted. "But I found my phone in her stuff. I saw the texts."

My grandmother tilted her head and looked at me, as though it was just dawning on her that her teenage granddaughter from three states away had unexpectedly arrived and was now sitting at her kitchen table. "How did you know she was here?"

I started to say she'd come to me in a dream, but I wasn't sure how Zoe would take it. "I remembered how we used to come here together when I was little," I said. "Somehow, I just knew this was where she'd go."

I took a sip of my tea. I felt warm and, for the first time in weeks, incredibly sleepy, almost too tired to form words. Maybe my grandmother had put something in my tea, too. My eyes started to close, my head falling forward.

"How long has my mom been asleep?" I asked groggily.

My grandmother glanced at the clock. "An hour?"

"I think I should go check on her," I said. "And then maybe I'll lie down for a minute."

• • •

My legs were heavy with fatigue as I started up the stairs to my grandmother's bedroom, and I leaned on the railing, pausing at each step.

Then I came to the pictures documenting my childhood, the pictures I usually tried not to look at because they made me terribly, inexplicably sad. But this time was different. This time I stopped and really looked.

The first two were standard-issue cute-kid shots: Me at Coney Island, holding a stick of cotton candy bigger than my head. Me offering a giraffe a piece of lettuce at the Bronx Zoo, neither of us looking particularly enthusiastic about the negotiation. Nothing to be afraid of.

Then I got to the last picture. Me sitting on my mom's lap, sucking my thumb, on the steps of my grandmother's cabin.

I was older in this picture, too old to be sucking my thumb. My hair, still all-black at the temples, was plastered to the sides of my head. My swimsuit sagged around my legs. My shoulder blades winged sharply. My mom leaned over me, cradling me in her arms, half her face hidden by her hair.

The day came back to me in a rush, and I was there, at the lake, with my mom.

We had swum out to the floating dock together. We were lying in the sun, all toasty and warm, dozing, with the shouts of the other families playing by the shore echoing off the mountains. I'd just drifted off to sleep when my mom picked up my foot, kissed the instep, and told me I was her magical girl. Then she stood and dived off the dock. But instead of heading back to shore, she started swimming toward the middle of the lake.

I sat up on the dock, wide awake. I called to her, tentatively at first, then louder. I jumped up and down, making the dock bobble on the surface of the lake, my throat growing raw. I waved my arms, yelling for help, but the swimmers playing by the shore just waved back. Her figure was getting smaller.

When I could just see the rise and scoop of her arms, I jumped in and began dog-paddling after her. I knew it was hopeless. She was a much stronger swimmer than I was, and with each stroke she increased her lead. Soon I was out too far to turn back. Panic snarled my legs like a rope around my ankles.

I tried once more to call out to her, and my mouth filled with lake water.

The next thing I knew I was being lifted up by the straps of my bathing suit and pulled roughly over the side of the rowboat. I lay on the floor of the boat, panting and coughing and sobbing, while my dad rowed. When he pulled up alongside my mom, she stopped swimming and turned to us, treading water, barely breathing hard.

Get in, my dad said in a voice strained with rage. She put her hands on the side of the boat and pulled herself in. My dad threw her a towel.

I was going to turn around, she said. *I just wanted to see how far I could get.*

I didn't look at her the whole way back, but when we were safe on shore I climbed onto her lap and wouldn't get off the rest of the afternoon. I knew that she'd been lying. In those few seconds of sleep on the dock, before she kissed my foot and called me her magical girl, then dived into the water, I'd dreamed everything that was to come.

In my dream she hadn't turned around.

• • •

I took the rest of the stairs two at a time, my heart knocking in my chest, my breath fast and ragged in my throat. I pushed open the door to my grandmother's room and gave the bed a quick glance to make sure it was empty. I checked the guest bedroom, too, then ran back down the stairs.

I grabbed Zoe by the arm and pulled her with me out of the house, down the porch steps, and together we half ran, half stumbled down the hill to the lake.

CHAPTER FORTY-SEVEN

The boat was in the middle of the lake, rocking gently. My mother was sitting with her back to us. She wasn't wearing a coat, and she had her arms wrapped around herself. She was rocking, too, back and forth, as the boat rocked side to side.

"Mom!" I yelled, jumping up and down. "Mom!"

"I don't think she can hear you," Zoe said. I started walking toward the water. A thin layer of lacy ice clung to the shore, and chunks of ice floated on the waves. In some places, the lake had already frozen through, and branches and leaves and small rocks sat scattered across the hard, dull surface.

I took a step into the water, breaking through the crust of ice. The cold was so intense I didn't feel it at first, just felt my breath ripped from my lungs.

"Don't." Zoe grabbed my arm. "It's too cold. You'll freeze to death."

"But so will she. I have to save her."

"Maybe she'll come back." Her grip was strong.

"She wants to die." I turned toward the lake. "Mom! Mommy!" I hadn't called her mommy in forever.

Just then she stood up, as though she'd heard me. But she didn't turn to us. She moved to the middle of the boat and stood, looking over the side.

She put one foot up on the side, getting ready.

I turned and grabbed Zoe's other arm, so that we were facing each other. "Do something," I begged, shaking her. "She's going to jump in. Please."

"What am I supposed to do?"

"You can help her. I know you can," I shouted.

Zoe's eyes grew enormous. Her whole body shivered once, like a seizure, then got very still. She shook free of my grip and turned toward the lake. Her face was clouded and distant with concentration. Heat radiated off her. She touched her mole, then closed her eyes.

Below the wind, I heard a low hum. I couldn't tell if it was coming from her mouth or her whole body. All at once the wind stopped and everything went quiet—so quiet, I could hear my mother inhale, taking a final lungful of air, preparing for the freezing blackness.

"Mommy!" I shouted again.

The boat shot out across the lake.

My mother fell backward into it.

The boat kept moving, not fast but deliberately toward the shore, the waves breaking steadily across its bow.

Zoe reached out her hand and I took it. It was warm and wet with sweat. We stood there holding hands as the boat moved across the lake toward us. When it was a few feet from the shore I dropped Zoe's hand and ran out into the water, grabbed the ring at the bow, and pulled the boat the rest of the way in.

My mother lay across the seat. Her lips were blue and her skin was very pale. There was a knot forming on the side of her forehead where she must have hit it when she fell in, and a small scrape, trickling blood into her hair. But she was breathing.

• • •

I climbed into the boat and took off my jacket and wrapped it around my mom, then pulled her head into my lap. After a minute she opened her eyes and looked up at me.

"Please don't leave us," I said. "Please stay."

"I've ruined everything." My mom pushed herself up to sit in the boat. She reached up and touched her head where she was bleeding. She started crying, her lips trembling and tears leaking from her eyes. "You and your dad would be so much better off without me."

"It's not true."

"It's my fault your friend's dead."

"I don't care. I don't care if it is your fault. It's bad enough that Tabitha's dead. It will only make things worse if you die, too."

She wrapped her arms around me and we clung to each other. At first her grip felt steely and sharp, as usual, but then she relaxed into me, neither letting go nor holding on too tight.

It was the best hug she'd ever given me, and I wanted it to last forever.

We might have stayed that way, too, hugging in a rowboat for the rest of the day, if we both hadn't become aware of a low, keening sound.

Zoe.

Wading into the lake.

Tears running down her face.

"It's not your fault," she said to my mom. "It's mine. I killed Tabitha."

And then she pitched herself forward and disappeared into the dark water.

CHAPTER FORTY-EIGHT

By the time my mom and I pulled Zoe out of the lake, she was so cold she barely struggled, and her eyes had a weird glassy look. We each put an arm around her and dragged her up to the cabin, her teeth chattering violently and her body shaking with shivery sobs. It was only after we got her inside and wrapped her in blankets and the color started coming back into her lips that I realized I was soaked and freezing, too.

My grandmother drove down the mountain to town to call my dad while Zoe, my mom, and I took turns taking hot showers. When we came down to the kitchen, we found a pot of stew warming on the stove and the bottle of raki on the table.

At first none of us could eat, and we just sat at the table, staring at each other. Both my mom and Zoe had dazed, punchy looks, like they couldn't believe what they'd just done or what the other had just tried to do. I probably looked pretty wild-eyed myself. Finally, my mom poured a shot of raki, pushed it in front of Zoe, and nodded for her to drink it.

"Why don't you go first," she said.

Zoe swallowed most of the raki in one gulp, took a breath, and began telling us what had happened the night of Amanda's party.

Jake had been right; the Carolines had never accepted Tabitha. Some, like the twins, didn't care about her either way. Amanda flat-out hated her. Zoe thought Tabitha was fine in small doses but was afraid to cross Amanda.

Other girls had tried to join their clique before, but none had been as determined or tenacious as Tabitha. The more they hinted she wasn't one of them, the harder she tried to fit in. They went to a new lunch place; she showed up. They changed subway cars; she was waiting for them on the platform when they got off. It was, Zoe said, like she had some power that made it impossible for them to shake her.

What, my mom asked, frowning, was so bad about her?

Zoe shrugged. There was nothing exactly *wrong* with her. It was just her eagerness to be their friend and her willed obliviousness to the fact the feeling was not mutual. It grated after a while. To Amanda especially, who was used to everyone doing exactly what she wanted. In a weird way, Tabitha's insistence that they were best friends was an act of defiance none of the other girls would've dared, and it drove Amanda crazy.

She was the one who came up with the plan.

At her party, she'd suggest they go to the pool. They'd be drinking, of course.

She'd text Jake and his buddies to meet them, saying she had a surprise for them.

She'd make sure Tabitha was drunk enough to not know what she was doing. She'd accomplish this by telling Tabitha that in order to be on the track team, she had to undergo an initiation ritual. The first part was drinking three shots of tequila in five minutes.

The second part was running ten laps around the pool, naked.

While Tabitha was running around the pool, Amanda and the rest of the girls would hide.

When the boys got there, they'd find Tabitha, naked and drunk, alone.

Surprise!

Whatever happened, Amanda would record it all with her phone.

By Monday, the video would be everywhere.

Maybe it would just be Tabitha, minus her clothes, making a fool of herself in front of the most popular boys in the school.

Maybe it would be way worse.

No matter what, it would teach her not to hang out where she wasn't wanted. Possibly she'd be so embarrassed she'd change schools. And she'd never know exactly who was responsible, because they'd all take a vow of silence.

Everything went according to plan. They started the party at Amanda's apartment, and Tabitha got tipsy off hard lemonade before they even left.

Tabitha drunk was even more annoying than sober, and by the time they got to the pool, Zoe was beginning to think the plan might actually be a good idea. She was sick of Tabitha, and even more than that, she was sick of listening to Amanda complain about Tabitha.

But then Tabitha gave Amanda a card she'd made her for her birthday.

When Zoe said this, I let out a little yelp. The thought of Tabitha making a card for someone else hurt. A lot. Zoe and my mom looked at me. "Hot," I said, fanning my mouth and pointing to my stew. I motioned for Zoe to go on.

Zoe started feeling bad when she saw the card. Did it have to happen this way? Couldn't they just talk to Tabitha, explain that she was better off without them? Being popular wasn't as amazing as everyone thought. Surely Tabitha would understand if they were just honest with her.

Then Tabitha started talking about me. She said I'd been texting her all night, but she'd told me she had her own friends now, and it was my fault we weren't friends anymore.

When Zoe heard that, she got really worried. Once she and Amanda dropped her, Tabitha would have no one. She'd given up her friendship with me for them, and now she was about to lose them, too. It wasn't fair. She hadn't done anything wrong.

All she'd wanted was to be popular.

Tabitha got another text and said she had to go outside for a minute to meet me. She said she'd get rid of me and come right back.

While Tabitha was gone, Zoe told Amanda maybe they should call the whole thing off. Amanda said it was too late; she'd already texted the guys. Besides, what was wrong with Zoe? Did she actually like Tabitha? Maybe she'd be happier being a loser, too. Tabitha could probably take her place on the track team . . .

Tabitha came back inside. She looked weird, dazed and spacey, like she'd seen a ghost.

I glanced at my mom, but she kept looking at Zoe.

Zoe was about to ask Tabitha what had happened outside when she got a text from Jake. He and his friends were on their way.

Amanda told Tabitha about the track initiation ritual. She got out the tequila. The other girls gathered around. Tabitha started doing shots, with the other girls cheering her on.

Zoe had to do something.

Then Amanda said it was time for Tabitha to strip and run laps around the pool.

Zoe knew it was now or never.

Tabitha was standing by the edge of the pool, fiddling with her belt.

Zoe looked at her. She had to help her. But how? She closed her eyes . . .

Abruptly, Zoe stopped talking and dropped her spoon. It clattered off the table to the floor. "And then I pushed her," Zoe said quietly. My mom bent down to pick up the spoon. Zoe and I stared at each other across the table. I raised my eyebrows. She gave me the tiniest hint of a smile, touched her mole, then looked away.

The rest of the girls would think Tabitha had jumped in, Zoe continued, as my mom wiped the spoon on her napkin and put it back by Zoe's bowl. It wasn't much, but it would change the course of the night's events, which were beginning to feel unstoppable. Maybe the cold water would sober Tabitha up a bit. Maybe more girls would jump in with their clothes on, too.

She heard the splash as Tabitha hit the water.

Just then Priya turned out the lights, and Imani and Isa came out of the locker room with a cake they'd baked for Amanda, and everyone started singing. Priya told Amanda to make a wish, and Amanda looked straight at Zoe and gave her a weird, cold stare. Then she took a deep breath and blew out all the candles.

Imani and Isa had forgotten forks and plates, so all the girls dug their hands into the cake, and then Amanda wiped her hands on Zoe's hair, and soon everyone was having a cake fight in the gloomy twilight of the cavernous, chlorine-scented room. By the time they'd stopped screaming and laughing and smearing cake on each other, they were all sticky and covered in chocolate frosting, and Priya said they really did need to go swimming, to clean off.

That's when Zoe realized Tabitha had never come up from falling in the water.

When they turned the lights back on, they saw her floating face-down, at the shallow end of the pool.

CHAPTER FORTY-NINE

"I'm so sorry, Tess," Zoe said, her voice cracking. "If I hadn't made her fall in the pool, she'd still be alive. But you have to believe me, I didn't do it to hurt her. I was trying to protect her. And maybe if we hadn't gotten distracted by the cake, we would have noticed her . . ." Tears rolled down her cheeks.

"It's not your fault. Well, maybe, partially, but not totally." I looked at my mom. "Right?"

"Right. If I hadn't asked her to come outside to meet me, she might not have been so upset, and maybe she wouldn't have done the tequila shots."

I stared at my mom, waiting.

"What?" she said.

"It wasn't just the tequila," I prompted.

"It wasn't?" my mom and Zoe said together.

"The coroner found drugs in her blood, too. You gave her drugs when she came outside, right?"

"You did?" Zoe gasped.

"Are you insane?" my mom shouted. She stopped, took a breath, then started again in a calmer voice. "I just wanted to talk to her. I told her how bad you felt, Tess, and I asked her to give you one more chance. I knew you were too proud, and too stubborn, to apologize for whatever you'd said to her on the phone."

"What did she say?" I asked, my voice small.

"She was upset. She said she thought it was too late for you to be friends again, but that she missed you. When she said that, she started to cry. I got her to promise to call you in the morning to at least talk about it, but I don't know, she was pretty shaken up when she went back inside. I never should have interfered, but I certainly didn't give her drugs. How could you have thought that?"

I looked down at my empty bowl. Zoe watched us. "I don't know. It didn't make sense, but you had been . . . not yourself . . . for a while when it happened. And I guess I haven't been myself either. I've been having a hard time knowing what's real and what's not. Who I can trust," I added, glancing at Zoe.

My mom reached over and touched my hand. "I didn't know what to do when I found out Tabitha died. I should have told you that I'd met her, but I was scared. It just seemed better for everyone if I disappeared for a while. And then they gave me such strong drugs at the hospital, it was easy to pretend the whole thing had been a dream."

"Wait," Zoe said. "If you didn't give Tabitha drugs, who did?"

I wished my grandmother were there, with her ability to see both the past and the future. She'd been gone for a long time. Maybe she was staying out on purpose to give us all a chance to talk.

I turned to Zoe.

"Do you remember anything else about what happened that night? You said Tabitha was acting weird when she came back from meeting my mom, and then Amanda told her about the initiation ritual, and then she did the shots of tequila and started getting undressed. Anything else?"

Zoe closed her eyes and scrunched her forehead, thinking. My mom and I sat quietly, waiting. I heard the tick of the clock above the stove. Finally Zoe opened her eyes.

"She was kinda weird when she came back, but now that I know what your mom said, maybe she was just sad. And she was eager to do the shots. And then Amanda told her about running the laps, and she started taking off her clothes."

"And that's it?" my mom asked.

"No, wait. First she went over to her backpack. I figured she was just putting her phone someplace safe, but maybe she had drugs in her backpack? Maybe she took them then?"

"Maybe." It didn't sound like Tabitha to have a secret stash of drugs in her backpack, but then what did I actually know about her? What did I know about any of us? I had been ready to believe my mom had given Tabitha drugs, ready to believe Zoe and Amanda had tried to frame me for her death.

I closed my eyes. I tried to picture Tabitha—the Tabitha I had known, with her frizzy hair, her round cheeks, her mouth slightly open, smiling and breathing hard . . .

I opened my eyes.

"Her inhaler. I bet she went over to her backpack to take a hit off her inhaler before running the laps." I got a flash of her bent over her open pack, sneaking a quick puff at the track practice.

"She had asthma?" Zoe said.

"She didn't want to people to know. She would have been embarrassed for any of you to see her using her inhaler. But she always had it with her."

"Do you think that had anything to do with what happened?" my mom asked.

"Maybe? The detective gave me his card. I'll call him as soon as we get back to New York." I looked at Zoe. "Will you tell him what you told us, about Amanda making Tabitha do the tequila shots and her plan to leave her alone with Jake and his friends?"

Zoe hesitated. She fiddled with her near-empty glass of raki, then lifted it to her mouth and drained it. "I will." She set the glass firmly on the table. "She made us all swear we'd say it was just a tragic accident, but it wasn't." She looked at me and then my mom. "If it was anyone's fault, it was Amanda's."

CHAPTER FIFTY

When my grandmother came back, she said my dad was taking the train up in the morning, and we'd all drive back in my mom's rental car. My grandmother looked small and wrinkled and worried, not at all powerful, not at all magical, just relieved to have everyone in the same room, alive, and exhausted by what it had taken to get us there.

Zoe looked small and tired, too, like talking about the night Tabitha drowned had made it real for her for the first time.

That night, we slept in the attic room, a very small, very pathetic slumber party.

"I'm sorry about your mom," Zoe whispered, once we'd turned out the lights and were lying in our beds. "I should have told you everything before."

"Probably. But you can't blame yourself for what happened to Tabitha. You were just trying to help her."

"I could have helped her more. I could have told her what Amanda was planning."

I stared up at the exposed beams of the ceiling, remembering the first time I'd had the vision of Tabitha's death, lying in this same bed at the end of the summer. "I could have helped her more, too."

We were both quiet.

I thought Zoe had fallen asleep when she whispered again. "It's not your fault, you know."

"It's not your fault, either."

"I don't just mean Tabitha. I mean what happened to Tabitha but also how people treat you at school. It's not fair, and you don't deserve it."

Tears streamed down my face onto my pillow. I opened my mouth to say something, but I didn't have any words.

After a while I felt a little better. "Zoe?" I whispered. "You didn't really push Tabitha into the pool with your hands. You used your mind to make her fall in, just like with the car crash and the basketball and the rowboat. I'm not crazy to think you have magic powers, right?"

A slight rustling came from Zoe's side of the room, and I held my breath, waiting for her answer. But she didn't say anything, and after a few more minutes I heard a gentle, regular rasp in her breath. Whether or not she'd heard my question, she'd fallen asleep.

Eventually I fell asleep, too, and if I had any dreams, they were gone when I woke up.

PART THREE

CHAPTER FIFTY-ONE

The last day of school before winter break, Ms. Labos called me into her office. When I'd shut the door and sat down on the sofa, she told me that after Zoe had told Detective O'Ryan what had happened at the pool, the lab had retested Tabitha's blood samples for asthma medication, and the test had come back positive. But the coroner said that while the asthma drugs might have interacted with the alcohol in Tabitha's system, there was also a chance it was the angle of the fall and the impact of her head against the bottom of the pool that had killed her, so it was impossible to assign blame. No criminal charges would be filed against Amanda or anyone.

Even so, Amanda wouldn't be coming back after the break. Her parents were sending her to a wilderness school for troubled teens, where she'd hike and take care of livestock and think about the role she'd played in Tabitha's death, as well as how she'd treated people in general over the past years.

When she said this last part, Ms. Labos looked at me expectantly. I knew I should feel happy that my nemesis was finally going to be out of my life, but I just felt empty. I would never forgive Amanda for what she'd done to Tabitha, for what she'd done to both of us.

As if reading my mind, Ms. Labos smiled. "For what it's worth, she feels very bad about what happened."

"Did she say that?"

"Well, she didn't take full responsibility. That's going to take some time. Not that it excuses what she did, but Amanda's had a tough time of it. I shouldn't be telling you this, but she's struggled a lot. I don't think either of her parents has been as involved as they could have been, so maybe this wilderness school will be the best thing."

"Maybe." I refused to feel sorry for Amanda. We'd all had a tough time. We'd all struggled.

"So, I hope you can start putting all this behind you over winter break and think of next semester as a new leaf," Ms. Labos continued. "You could come back and find everything's changed, you know."

"I could come back a completely normal person?" I asked, quoting *Sixteen Candles*.

Ms. Labos gave me a little smile. "Yep. But I hope you don't. Being a Caroline's not all it's cracked up to be."

CHAPTER FIFTY-TWO

Zoe texted a few times in the first week of break, seeing if I wanted to hang out. I guess with Amanda gone she was panicking about who she would be friends with once school started again. Maybe she still felt guilty about her role in Tabitha's death. Or maybe she truly did think we had a connection.

I said I needed to stay home with my dad and my mom. My mom had agreed to go back into the hospital to try something called ECT, where they shock your brain out of being depressed. It sounds awful, but the doctors said they'd had a lot of luck with it with patients like her who didn't respond well to medication.

In the meantime, we were staying in a lot, both because I think none of us was sure what she would be like after the treatment and because we were worried what she might do if we left her on her own.

• • •

I went for long runs every day over break. My legs snapped back into shape quickly, and I felt like I might be even faster than when I'd stopped, like maybe the time off had been good for me. I was looking forward to practice starting in the spring. Even if Coach didn't let me compete, it would be good to be running with the team again.

On Christmas morning I woke up and spent some time examining my streak in the mirror, trying to decide if more strands had turned white. Jujube lay on my bed, watching me. He had been quiet the past few days, but when I looked at him, he blinked, then twitched his nose.

Merry Christmas.

"Thanks," I whispered. "Merry Christmas, Juju," but he had gone back to licking his tail.

The rest of the day was quiet. If Tabitha had been alive, I would have gone over to her apartment in the afternoon to compare presents and eat gingerbread cookies. I tried not to think about Katie alone with the tree this year, if she even got one.

• • •

By New Year's Eve, I was sick of hanging out with my parents every day, so when Zoe texted, saying Jake's parents were out of town and I *had* to go to a party at his apartment with her that night, I agreed.

I'll admit, I was looking forward to seeing Jake again.

I told my parents I was going on a walk and went to some stores, looking for a new outfit. I even tried on a few pairs of skinny jeans that were so tight I had to jump up and down to pull them up. There was a spray tan place next door, and a salon up the block that did hair straightening. I had my dad's in-case-of-emergency credit card. But it didn't feel like an emergency.

That night, I stood in front of the mirror in my same old saggy-butt jeans, same old faded black hoodie, same old stinky Converse. I unzipped my hoodie past my collarbones and rubbed some gloss on my lips and brushed my hair.

I looked fine.

I looked like myself.

CHAPTER FIFTY-THREE

Jake's apartment was big and dark and crowded. There was a keg and red plastic cups, and the furniture had been pushed against the walls and the carpet rolled up to expose the bare floors. Eli and a bunch of guys his age stood around in button-down shirts roaring at each other, while their girlfriends perched on the back of the sofa, taking little sips from their cups, looking mortified to have found themselves at a high school party, like if they accidentally brushed against one of us they would be hurtled back in time to the eleventh grade.

Zoe found me and gave me a beer and pulled me over to where she was talking with the twins and Jake and a guy named Jayden who went to a different school.

Amanda wasn't there, of course.

Jake and Jayden were talking about the latest *Saw* movie, describing the most disgusting scenes, while Zoe and Imani and Isa screamed and covered their ears. I stood there listening for a while, trying to look interested.

If Tabitha had been there, she would've screamed and squealed along with Zoe and the twins. When Jayden said the *Saw* movies were awesome, she would have said, *Totally awesome!* and then if, five minutes later, Imani or Isa said they were stupid, she would have nodded and said, *Right, so stupid.*

She would've finished her beer and asked for a refill. While Jayden went back to the keg, she would've pulled me into the bathroom so she could reapply her lip gloss and strategize about how to get Jayden to talk to her and debate whether she should wear her hair in a ponytail, or down, or maybe a messy bun on top of her head?

It would've been one of the best nights of her life.

I drifted over to a window that wasn't occupied by cigar smokers and looked out at the city. Down on the avenue, people in New Year's Eve hats were walking in clumps, laughing and shouting between groups and stepping into the middle of the street to try to hail cabs.

There were so many more people on all the other streets just in Manhattan alone, not to mention the world.

All of them strangers.

I'd never have a friend like Tabitha again. She had been nice to me when no one else had. She had accepted me for exactly who I was. Maybe we hadn't had much in common besides both being outcasts, and maybe she was kind of obnoxious. But Tabitha hadn't been just my only friend, she had been a good one.

It struck me that she wasn't just missing the stuff that was happening this year—things like the track team sleepover at Zoe's, or this party, or even the prom—especially the prom, if she'd been serious about wanting to go. She was going to miss what should have been the rest of her life.

Up to this point, I'd felt sad about her death mostly because of what it meant for me. It meant that everything that happened to me from now on, everything I did, I'd be doing on my own. Sometimes life felt so hard, so lonely, so confusing, I could understand why my mom wanted to give up. And if I knew for sure I was going to be crazy like her, I might have given up, too.

But I wasn't like my mom, at least not yet. Lonely and confusing as life was, I'd still choose it over the alternative. Tabitha no longer had that choice. For the first time, I was sad not for myself but for her.

She shouldn't have died.

She should've been here.

48, 47, 46 . . .

I wiped my eyes and turned from the window. Back in the party, someone turned down the music, and everyone joined the count toward midnight.

Zoe was standing by Jake, tossing her hair and swaying to the countdown. When they got to ten, she put her arms around him and he leaned down and they started making out.

I looked away.

When I looked back, his eyes were open and he was staring straight at me.

"Happy New Year!" everyone yelled and started kissing and hugging each other.

I just stood there, staring at Jake.

He raised his eyebrows at me, and I raised mine back, then felt my face flush and my mouth go dry. I put down my beer and pushed my way out of the room, suddenly feeling very hot and lightheaded.

• • •

Upstairs, I opened a door and heard a "Hey!" and the scuffling of sheets from the middle of the room.

"Sorry!" I yelped, pulling the door shut.

I tried another door. The room was empty, so I went in.

Enough light came in through the window for me to find the lamp on the desk and turn it on. There was a single bed and a desk with a sewing machine with a plastic cover over it, a basket of scraps of material on the floor, a bookcase. A crocheted teddy bear in a Whitman Day jersey sat propped against the pillows on the bed. The wall above the bed was covered with posters of Alex Rodriguez and Mike Piazza, and curling clippings from the *New York Post* listing the scores of high school basketball games.

One full-page clipping had a blurry photo of a kid going in for a lay-up. I peered at it and saw that it was a thinner, younger, fuller-haired Eli. This must have been his bedroom, now a half shrine to his high school glory, half graveyard for his mom's unfinished hobbies.

I moved over to the bookcase, curious about what Eli would have read when he was my age. Not surprisingly, his taste ran heavily toward science fiction and international spy thrillers. The lower shelf was stacked with his high school yearbooks. I pulled down the most recent one, from when he'd been a senior, six years ago.

Already the clothes and haircuts looked incredibly dumb. I imagined Eli pulling the book off the shelf and cringing at his former self, just the way, six years from now, Zoe and the rest would be mortified to see how they used to dress, what they used to think was cool.

I flipped forward to the superlatives. Most Likely to Succeed: Eli Boylan. Of course. Most Athletic: again, Eli Boylan. Most Likely to Call You in Ten Years to "Make Amends": Eli Boylan. It took me a second to figure that one out. Cutest Couple: Eli Boylan and Heather Labos. Most Likely to Say She Goes to School "Near Boston": Heather Labos. Best Dancer . . .

I stopped and went back to Cutest Couple. Eli Boylan and . . . Heather Labos? As in Ms. Labos? As in the biggest natural-born nerd I'd ever seen?

I carried the yearbook over to the desk lamp. It was her. Skinnier, with rounder cheeks and longer hair, but definitely Ms. Labos, posing with her arms wrapped around Eli's neck.

I turned the page and there the two of them were, homecoming king and queen. Ms. Labos—Heather—had gone out with Eli Boylan.

Ms. Labos—Heather—had been a Caroline.

I sat for a long time looking at the picture of Ms. Labos—
Heather—and Eli. No wonder she had acted so weird at Papaya
Dog that day. They must have been the Zoe and Jake of their
class. She had been popular and pretty and smart, half of a perfect
couple; she probably thought the rest of her life would be perfect,
too. She'd gone away to college but then, for whatever reason,
she'd come back home and now lived with her parents and was a
high school guidance counselor with a weakness for fast food.

Who you were in high school wasn't who you were forever.

Change was possible.

Anything could happen.

No one knew what the future held.

Not even Zoe.

Not even me.

CHAPTER FIFTY-FOUR

Chronologically, you're sixteen today. Physically, you're still fifteen.

"Hang on, before we start, who wants soda?" Katie paused the movie. It was February 13, Tabitha's birthday, and Katie, my mom, and I were sitting uncomfortably on Tabitha's bed, watching *Sixteen Candles*.

We'd just gotten to the scene at the beginning of the movie where Samantha wakes up and examines herself in the mirror to see if she looks any different now that she's a year older.

I would have thought Katie would want to mark Tabitha's birthday with a big public thing at the school, all the popular girls releasing balloons or doves or something, but she'd called a week earlier and said what she thought Tabitha would have wanted was to watch her favorite movie with her best friend.

I didn't correct her and say *former best friend.*

I just said okay, but that my mom would have to come, too. Her ECT treatments had been going well, but there was still a chance of seizure as a side effect, which meant she couldn't be left alone for too long in case she swallowed her tongue or something.

My mom and I had passed the community room on our way to the elevators. The Ping-Pong table was still there, but the net had been torn, and the surface of the table was warped and ringed with white circles where people had put wet glasses.

When my mom saw it, she gave a little smile and shook her head. In that gesture, I saw how hard it must have been for her to know that I'd rather spend my time at my friend's apartment, with my friend's mom, than home with her.

How embarrassed I was by her.

How much I wanted her to be something—someone—she couldn't.

She'd bought the Ping-Pong table in hopes that it would make our apartment a little bit more like Tabitha's, since she couldn't make herself more like Katie. I wanted to tell her that I'd never wished Katie were my mom, that Tabitha hadn't been any happier than I had.

That I was sorry.

"Ping-Pong's a stupid game," I said.

"Idiotic," my mom agreed and gave my shoulder a squeeze. Her grip was still too strong, but I didn't mind.

• • •

Without waiting for us to answer, Katie ran out of the room and came back with Diet Cokes for everyone. She was acting super nervous, like she wanted to be sure she was being a good hostess. Maybe she was uncomfortable with my mom there. Maybe she wasn't sure what to say to me.

Or maybe she just missed Tabitha and was doing her best to hide it with all her bustling around.

We watched in silence for a while. Without Tabitha there, it felt wrong to say the lines along with the movie, but it was almost like watching without the sound on. I looked at Katie and saw her lips moving, but she was staring at the screen and didn't even notice I was watching her.

My mom sat quietly. I couldn't tell if she liked the movie or thought it was dumb or was having a hard time following it. The ECT made her a little slow sometimes. The doctors said it would get better once her brain adjusted.

I hadn't watched the movie in months, and seeing it again was like hearing the lines for the first time.

When it got to the scene in the auto shop, where Samantha tells Ted he could come back in the fall as a completely normal person, I must have made a little noise, because both my mom and Katie looked at me. I put my hand over my mouth and said, "Excuse me," pretending I'd burped.

They didn't know that this was where it had all begun.

That night less than a year earlier, when Tabitha had paused the movie, thrown away the Oreos, and decided to change her life. *Don't do it*, I wanted to say to Ted. *Don't change a thing.*

A year ago, I'd have said *Sixteen Candles* is about wanting to fit in. Now I saw it was about wanting to grow up. Wanting to look older, feel older. There's a scene where Caroline says to Jake, *I fantasize that I'm your wife, and we're the richest, most popular adults in town.* But in real life does being an adult make you any happier than you were as a kid? Maybe sometimes. But not for my mom. Not for Katie.

The movie's also about how growing up means your parents don't take care of you anymore, but maybe, also, you don't have to take care of them. At the end of the movie, when Jake comes to meet Samantha at her sister's wedding, he says, *Do you have to go to the reception now?* At first she says, *Yes*, but then she says, *No*. She doesn't have to follow her family. She can go with Jake. She can lead her own life. As she's getting into Jake's car, her dad sees her and gives her a big smile and a thumbs up.

I could only hope, when it was time for me to go my own way, my dad would be as cool about it.

• • •

At the end of the movie, when Jake gives Sam the cake he's gotten for her and says, *Happy birthday, Samantha*, Katie whispered, "Happy birthday, Tabitha," and started to cry. My mom put her arm around Katie's shoulder and patted her awkwardly while the end credits rolled and Thompson Twins sang "If You Were Here."

If you were here, I could deceive you.
And if you were here, you would believe.
But would you suspect my emotion wandering? Yeah
Do not want a part of this anymore.

It was the saddest song in the world.

After a few minutes Katie sat up straight, disentangled herself from my mom, and said, "Cake?"

She brought in the cake and we sang "Happy Birthday" to Tabitha, fast and mumbly, none of us making eye contact. If she'd been there, Tabitha would've been seventeen. Instead, like Samantha, she'd stay sixteen forever.

It must have been hard for Katie to watch the movie. She was the one who'd shown it to Tabitha and me the first time. I remembered how, when we'd watched it, she'd told us about how much she loved it when she was in high school. She was already excited then for Tabitha to get older, to be a teenager so they could gossip about boys and clothes and the popular girls, and of course, the prom. High school had been the best time of Katie's life; she must've assumed she'd get to live it all again through her daughter.

I put down my fork and took a breath. "I'm really sorry, Katie," I said.

She'd been poking at her plate with her fork, pulling the icing away from the cake and mushing it into a paste, but now she stopped and looked at me. "What do you mean? What happened was an accident. A tragic . . ." She stopped, swallowed, and gave a little wag of her head, shaking off the cliché. "A *dumb, horrible* accident."

"I mean, I'm sorry I wasn't a better friend to Tabitha. I could have gone along with her plan to try to be more popular, to have more friends. I could have been more fun to begin with. I could have listened to what she was trying to tell me last summer, when she said she wanted to change."

I'd been thinking a lot about what Tabitha had said to me on the phone the night she died, that I never listened to what people were saying, only the way they said it. She'd been right. I hadn't listened when she'd told me why she wanted to be popular; I hadn't heard how unhappy she was. It must have been easier for Tabitha to act spazzy and hyper and bubbly than to admit how alone she felt, to acknowledge that even her best friend didn't know her. That neither of us really knew each other at all. I swallowed and looked at my plate.

"I'm sorry I didn't warn her about what was going to happen at the pool."

It was the first time I'd said it out loud, and I held my breath, waiting to hear what my mom and Katie would say. Would they laugh it off? Would they tell me I was crazy? But Katie just patted me vaguely on the knee.

"I know, Tesser." Her voice was quavery, and her eyes were leaking tears again. "I never should have let her go to that party."

My mom was watching us. "Actually, I've been meaning to ask. The text you sent Tabitha, the one about a crazy dream you'd had. Was it just a quote from the movie, or was it something else?"

I looked at my mom.

I looked at Katie.

I considered explaining the new theory I had, one I'd been working on during my long runs to the lighthouse and back. My theory was, we all had magical abilities. Zoe could make things move with her mind. Amanda could make people be meaner than they actually were. Tabitha could force someone to be friends with her, whether the person wanted to or not. I could see the future.

Maybe Ms. Labos had magical abilities when she was our age, too, and that's how she got Eli to be her boyfriend.

Maybe all teenagers have them. As you get older, you either lose them and become normal, like Katie, or else you keep them and go crazy, like my mom.

I knew what my mom and Katie would say about my theory. Katie would say I needed to stop blaming myself for Tabitha's death. My mom would say I'd been spending too much time with my grandmother.

Maybe.

And my dreams?

They'd say I'd won the race because that day, at that time, I was the fastest runner on the course.

That Finn had crashed the car because he'd been drinking and was driving too fast, and Zoe pushed the wheel.

That the basketball slipped out of Jake's hands.

They'd say I'd seen Tabitha drown in my dream because some secret part of me wanted her to.

That I'd dreamed my mom was going to try to kill herself because I knew she wanted to.

They'd say I was just an ordinary girl with a sick but nice mom and an overwhelmed but nice dad. An ordinary girl who was good at running and grammar, bad in social situations, and in need of a new best friend.

That Zoe was just lonely and scared in her own way and felt like as much of a freak as I did, even though she was Queen of the Carolines.

Maybe they'd be right.

My mom was still waiting for me to tell her what I'd meant when I'd texted Tabitha about my dream.

"Don't you know?" I smiled. "I'm your magical, magical girl."